Jessica rode the wave all the way to the beach and found herself running into Christian's arms. He picked her up and twirled her around, her wet body close against his. Suddenly they were kissing passionately, madly, as Jessica had never kissed anyone before. All she could hear was the pounding of the surf in the distance and the beating of her heart against his.

When Jessica finally pulled away, her stomach coiled. She felt as though nothing would ever be the same again. And the feeling scared her. How could she have such strong emotions for Christian when she was supposed to be in love with Ken?

The thrill of surfing is affecting me—that's all, Jessica reassured herself. But as Christian's smoky blue eyes burned into her, she knew deep down that she'd fallen in love.

IN LOVE WITH
THE ENEMY

Written by
Kate William

Created by
FRANCINE PASCAL

BANTAM BOOKS
NEW YORK · TORONTO · LONDON · SYDNEY · AUCKLAND

RL 6, age 12 and up

IN LOVE WITH THE ENEMY
A Bantam Book / January 1996

Sweet Valley High® *is a registered trademark of Francine Pascal*
Conceived by Francine Pascal
Produced by Daniel Weiss Associates, Inc.
33 West 17th Street
New York, NY 10011
Cover art by Bruce Emmett

ISBN: 0-553-56638-5

Published simultaneously in the United States and Canada

Bantam Books are published by Bantam Books, a division of Bantam
Doubleday Dell Publishing Group, Inc. Its trademark, consisting of the
words "Bantam Books" and the portrayal of a rooster, is Registered in
U.S. Patent and Trademark Office and in other countries. Marca
Registrada. Bantam Books, 1540 Broadway, New York, New York 10036.

PRINTED IN THE UNITED STATES OF AMERICA

OPM   0 9 8 7 6 5 4 3 2 1

To William Benjamin Rubin

Chapter 1

"Go, Gladiators!" sixteen-year-old Jessica Wakefield yelled, leaping up and waving her red-and-white pom-poms in the air. She was standing with her cocaptain, Heather Mallone, in front of the cheerleading squad, leading the girls in a series of spirited cheers at the football game against the Palisades Pumas on Friday evening.

The Palisades coach signaled a time-out and ran onto the field. While the two teams huddled, Jessica and Heather quickly conferred with the rest of the squad. They had spent all week choreographing new cheers for the game, and they were eager to try them out.

"Let's do 'Smokin,' the new rap routine," Amy Sutton suggested, her slate-gray eyes flashing with excitement. Turning her baseball cap around on her blond head, she strutted like a rap

1

singer and pointed an index finger at the girls.

"Girl, you're *smokin'*," Maria Santelli said.

All the girls laughed and Jessica grinned. She and Amy had written the lyrics to the cheer together, transforming the words of a popular rap song.

"'Smokin'' is our best," Jessica said. "Why don't we save that for halftime?"

"You're right," Amy agreed. "We shouldn't waste it now."

"How about our new salsa cheer?" Heather suggested.

Jessica nodded and clapped her hands sharply. "OK, girls, get in position for the 'Miami Sound Machine,'" she said.

"Play ball!" yelled the announcer.

Jessica clicked on the sound system as the players on the field trotted back into position. The funky opening notes of a Spanish song blasted through the air, and the girls fanned out into a V, taking position at arm's length from one another. Holding their hands in the air like Miami dancers, they waved their hips and moved their feet, shaking and prancing to the beat.

As the final drum beats brought the song to a finish, Jessica and Heather ran in front of the girls and crossed in simultaneous front handsprings. The rest of the girls leaped up in succession in double herkies and went down to the ground in side-by-side splits, creating the effect of an undulating wave.

As the girls raised their arms in the air, Jessica paused for breath, her cheeks flushed from exertion. She wound her silky golden-blond hair on top of her head and tied it in a knot, fanning the back of her neck with her hand. The air was hot and thick in the crowded football stadium, and beads of perspiration were dripping down her neck.

Heather glanced over at her. "Jess, take a break," she mouthed.

Jessica smiled gratefully at Heather. Her arms ached and her voice was hoarse from yelling. Usually Jessica and Heather competed for attention, but today they were working together. This was one of the most important games of the season. The Palisades Pumas were notorious rivals of Sweet Valley High, and the Gladiators needed all the support they could get.

Heather clapped her hands and ran in front of the girls. "Be aggressive, be, be aggressive!" she called.

Jessica sat down on the bench as the girls broke into the familiar "Aggressive" cheer, wiping the back of her neck with a towel. She picked up a plastic water bottle and took a long swig, taking in the action of the fast-paced game. She didn't remember when she'd seen such an exciting competition. The Sweet Valley Gladiators were in top form, but the Pumas had matched them play by play, and the score was tied.

Suddenly a cheer went through the crowd as

3

Jessica's boyfriend, Ken Matthews, took off down-field in a quarterback sneak. Ken was captain and star quarterback of the football squad. Jessica's heart swelled with pride as she watched her agile boyfriend run with the ball. He was tall and well built, with thick sandy-blond hair and cornflower-blue eyes. Jessica always thought Ken was one of the handsomest guys she'd ever seen. But he looked especially cute in his football uniform as he gripped the ball in the crook of his arm and dodged his opponents.

Jessica felt a surge of energy jolt through her body as she watched Ken run with the ball. She bounded up to join Heather in front of the girls.

"Ken, Ken, he's our man!" Jessica yelled.

"If he can't do it, nobody can!" Heather cried.

Jessica kept a sharp eye on her boyfriend as the rest of the cheerleaders picked up the chant. Ken was at his best today and had already scored two touchdowns. But Palisades was going strong. They were also playing rough. Bryce Fisherman, one of the Sweet Valley High halfbacks, had already been injured. He had been running with the ball when three massive linebackers had converged on him at once. His helmet had flipped off and he had flown to the turf, smashing his head on the ground. Jessica shuddered thinking about it. She had never seen such a violent tackle.

The announcer's voice boomed through the stadium. "The Gladiators' quarterback has been chased out of the pocket. He's running to the right. One man between him and the goal line! He fakes to the left, dives over the goal line, and . . . *touch-down!* Sweet Valley is in the lead!"

The Sweet Valley High fans leaped to their feet, cheering wildly.

Waving her pom-poms in the air, Jessica jumped up with the rest of her squad, all of them cheering in perfect unison.

During the Palisades' next possession, the quarterback passed the ball to his wide receiver. The Gladiators fans stomped on the bleachers with their feet, rocking the entire stadium. "De-fense, de-fense, de-fense!" they chanted.

A cry went through the crowd as Ricky Ordway, the cornerback of the Gladiators, leaped up and intercepted the ball. He faked a lateral and dodged the Puma receiver, sprinting across the field. Suddenly a burly Palisades lineman tackled him brutally. Ricky fumbled the ball and went down hard, grabbing his knee and rolling on the ground in pain.

Jessica's mouth dropped open, and she stared at the girls on the squad in shock. They all stopped cheering as they watched the commotion on the field.

"They're acting like savages," Amy said, falling onto the bench in disgust.

"That's giving them too much credit," Jean West said, pacing the width of the bench. "They're not even human. They're like wild beasts."

Jeanie's right, Jessica thought. The Palisades team wasn't playing like normal competitors. No wonder they were called Pumas. They were acting like a pack of hungry tigers fighting for a piece of raw meat. The Gladiators were their prey, and the Palisades Pumas were ripping them to shreds.

Ricky struggled to his feet, but his knee went out on him and he stumbled to the turf.

The referee signaled time-out and blew his whistle.

Coach Schultz ran out to the field and knelt by Ricky's side. Moments later he led the limping cornerback to the bench. The referee gave the Pumas only a five-yard penalty.

Jessica threw her pom-poms to the ground in disgust. "I can't believe this," she said. "That's the second guy out this half."

"They're playing dirty," Heather said, crossing her arms over her chest.

Jessica's blue-green eyes glittered angrily. "They're playing to kill."

"Wow, the stands are packed," Elizabeth Wakefield said to her best friend, Enid Rollins, as they made their way through the crowded stadium. It was halftime, and she and Enid had just arrived. Elizabeth was a writer for *The Oracle*, the school newspaper, and she had had to stay late for a staff meeting after school. She and Enid had stopped at

6

the concession stand first, for hot dogs and drinks. The band was playing the school song, and the Sweet Valley cheerleaders were in the middle of the field, rousing the crowd with a lively cheer.

"This is the biggest turnout we've had all year," Enid said, taking a bite out of her hot dog.

Elizabeth scanned the bleachers for a place to sit. Every seat was taken. It looked as if everyone from Sweet Valley High had turned out for the game. And they all seemed to be dressed in the school colors. The stands looked like a sea of red and white. "There's not a single spot free," she said.

"Oh, well, I guess we can't stay," Enid said. "Looks like we'll have to go to a movie instead." She glanced down at her watch. "If we hurry, we can still catch the new art film at the Plaza Theatre."

"Enid, c'mon," Elizabeth protested. "We've got to show some school spirit."

Enid took a sip of her soda. "Well, then, we're going to have to sit on someone's lap."

"Maybe Todd is here," Elizabeth said. "He told me he'd save seats for us if he got here in time." Todd Wilkins was Elizabeth's longtime steady boyfriend.

Enid looked at her in surprise. "He must be here," she said. "This is the most important game of the season."

"He's getting his cast off, but he was hoping to make it in time to catch some of the game,"

Elizabeth explained. Todd had broken his ankle during an important basketball game and had been in a walking cast for the last few weeks.

Enid peered into the crowd. "There's Winston," she said, pointing into the stands at a goofy-looking guy with a red-and-white Gladiators cap on. Elizabeth followed her gaze. Winston Egbert was sitting with Bruce Patman and Aaron Dallas. They were holding up a banner that read GLADIATORS RULE!

"Oh, well, I guess Todd's not here yet," Elizabeth said. "I don't see him anywhere."

"Looks like we're going to have to sit with the Palisades fans," Enid replied.

As the two girls made their way around the stands, the cheerleaders ran out to the middle of the field for their halftime show. The crowd greeted their appearance enthusiastically, whistling and hooting wildly.

"Look, that area's almost deserted," Enid said, pointing up into the bleachers on the Palisades side. They climbed up several rungs and made their way across a row of occupied seats.

"Excuse me," Elizabeth apologized, inching past two girls to a free spot. She took a seat next to a redheaded girl.

The redheaded girl did a double take as Elizabeth sat down. "I thought you were cheering," she said. She looked down to the field and back. "Is that your twin?"

"Yes, that's my sister, Jessica," Elizabeth said with a smile, holding out her hand. "I'm Elizabeth Wakefield, and this is Enid Rollins."

"I'm Marla Daniels," the girl introduced herself, shaking Elizabeth's hand. She had wild, curly auburn hair wrapped in a blue bandanna, smooth white skin, and sparkling green eyes. When she smiled, two tiny dimples appeared in her cheeks.

"Caitlin Alexander," her friend said, giving Elizabeth a friendly smile. She was tall and slender, with extremely short, choppy, straight black hair, almond-shaped brown eyes, and olive-colored skin. She was wearing two tiny silver hoops in her left ear.

Suddenly their attention was drawn to the field, where the cheerleaders were putting on their show.

"We've got the fever, we're hot, we can't be stopped," Jessica yelled, leading the girls in a dance number.

As the music segued into a rock beat, Jessica put on a solo performance. She skipped to the middle of the field, doing a series of front handsprings and one-armed cartwheels. Running to gain momentum, she leaped into the air in a perfect triple herky and came down for a landing in the splits, her arms held up in an L formation. The crowd hooted and hollered in appreciation.

Jessica is at her best tonight, Elizabeth thought, sitting back and taking a bite of her hot dog. *She's got the whole crowd revved up.*

Jessica grabbed the microphone. "Thank you!"

9

she yelled. "For our last number, we'd like to do a new rap routine. We call it 'Smokin'.' So let's get fired up to win!"

The crowd cheered and a popular rap beat filled the air. Jessica waited four beats, then began chanting rhythmically into the mike, tapping her foot on the ground. "SVH is smokin' / You know we ain't jokin' . . ."

Elizabeth covered her ears and groaned. "If I hear that song one more time, I think I'm going to spontaneously combust," she muttered to Enid.

Enid laughed. "Rap is Jessica's latest, huh?" she asked.

Elizabeth nodded. "And that means it's *my* latest, too," she groaned. Jessica's and Elizabeth's bedrooms were separated only by an adjoining bathroom, so Elizabeth was forced to share in Jessica's rapidly changing fads. Jessica had been driving her crazy all weekend blasting rap music and making up cheers with Amy. Elizabeth had been forced to listen to classical music through her headphones in order to get some writing done. She must have heard "Smokin'" about a hundred times in the last week. She had even heard it in her sleep and had incorporated it into her dreams.

Elizabeth fished around in her bag and pulled out last week's edition of *The Oracle*, trying to shut out the music from her thoughts. She crossed her legs and leaned back, skimming the contents of the school newspaper.

Caitlin glanced from Jessica to Elizabeth. "Looks like you two are twins in appearance only," she observed.

"You're right about that," Elizabeth said with a smile. Physically, she and Jessica were identical. They both had shoulder-length golden-blond hair, beautiful heart-shaped faces, and sparkling blue-green eyes. But that's where the similarities ended. The twins were completely different in character. From their taste in music, to their preference of clothes, to their choice of activities, Jessica and Elizabeth were like night and day. Jessica liked rap and rock; Elizabeth preferred jazz and classical music. Jessica wore daring miniskirts and strategically ripped jeans; Elizabeth wore casual khakis and polo shirts. Jessica's favorite activities were dancing, shopping, and scamming on guys; Elizabeth's were reading, writing poetry and articles for the school newspaper, and spending time with her boyfriend, Todd.

Elizabeth sighed as the players trotted out onto the field for the second half of the game. She wasn't really interested in football. She would have rather gone to the movie with Enid. But everybody had talked about the game all week in school, and Elizabeth wanted to show her support. Palisades had beaten Sweet Valley High twice in a row, and the Gladiators were determined to break their losing streak.

Elizabeth looked down at the field and tried to

11

take an interest in the game but found her attention wandering. Since she and Jessica had got back from their trip to Sweet Valley University, Elizabeth had been kind of depressed. The previous week she and Jessica had visited their brother, Steven, and his girlfriend, Billie Winkler, at SVU. Their parents had given them the vacation as a chance to get a feel for college life.

And we really got a feel for it, Elizabeth reflected, thinking back to the whirlwind they had experienced on the SVU campus. It had started out with a blast—literally—when Jessica had insisted on throwing a huge party behind Steven's back their first night there. Jessica thought the party was a huge success. Elizabeth thought it was a disaster. They had trashed the apartment, and the police had shown up at four in the morning.

But the evening hadn't been a total waste. At the party Elizabeth had met Ian Cooke, a journalism major. He had invited her to sit in on a seminar given by Professor Felicia Newkirk, a world-renowned journalist. Elizabeth had written a prize-winning essay in the journalism class and had been offered an internship with a nationally distributed newspaper. She had felt as if magic doors were suddenly opening before her. At the age of sixteen, she was being invited to work on a national newspaper under the tutelage of a famous journalist.

Then Elizabeth had made a major life decision. She had decided to take her high school equivalency exam and start college early. Not one to allow her twin sister to leave her behind, Jessica had quickly made up her mind to join Elizabeth at SVU. She had started rushing the most exclusive sorority on campus and had begun dating a college guy. But Elizabeth's internship had turned out to be nothing more than slave labor, and Jessica's college boyfriend had turned out to be a masquerading high-school student. So the twins had come home. Elizabeth was thrilled to be with her friends and family again, but her return felt anticlimactic. Compared to the excitement of the Sweet Valley University campus, high school was dullsville.

Elizabeth stifled a yawn as a Sweet Valley player made a touchdown and the crowd leaped to their feet.

Marla laughed. "Looks like you're not into football, either," she said.

"Not really," Elizabeth agreed. "Sports aren't my thing. Journalism is more up my alley."

"Me, too," Marla said. "I'm the editor of our school paper, and Caitlin is the arts editor."

"You're kidding!" Elizabeth exclaimed. "I write a weekly column for our paper." Then she paused in thought. "Actually, I've heard of your paper. Wasn't your staff written up recently in one of the community papers?"

Marla nodded. "We won a prize for 'Quality Reporting.' We've got a really good stable of writers," she added.

"We may have a great staff, but, unfortunately, we've got nothing to report on," Caitlin lamented.

"I know what you mean," Elizabeth said. "There's nothing going on here. Our last feature was about a teachers' conference."

"Ours was a PTA bake sale," Marla said.

Elizabeth laughed. "When you start covering brownies, you know you're in trouble."

"Well, they say that no news is good news," Enid put in.

"Not for journalists," Caitlin said ruefully.

"I know!" Elizabeth exclaimed, suddenly struck with an idea. "Why don't we *make* some news?"

"That's a great idea!" Caitlin enthused.

The girls put their heads together and brain-stormed for a while, looking for inspiration.

"How about a triathlon?" Marla suggested.

Caitlin's eyes lit up. "We could have an all-day sporting event for students from both schools."

Elizabeth groaned. All anyone had been discussing for the past week was the big game against the Palisades Pumas. And all Todd had been talking about was basketball, beginning every sentence with the phrase, "When I get my cast off . . ." Elizabeth couldn't wait for him to get his cast off. Then she wouldn't have to hear about it every five minutes.

"Please," Elizabeth said, holding her hand above her head. "I've had it up to here with sports."

"Yeah, we're a little sported-out at the moment," Enid agreed.

"Well, then, maybe we should do some kind of literary activity," Caitlin suggested.

Elizabeth pondered the idea. "How about a poetry-reading night?" she said. When she had been at SVU, she and Ian had attended a poetry reading at the campus coffee bar. A German student had read a haunting poem about the Berlin Wall, and the conversation afterward had been fascinating.

"Or just a literary night," Marla said. "You know, where students could read any of their material—poems or short stories or essays."

But Enid was shaking her head. "Personally, I think it sounds like a great idea," she said, "but, unfortunately, I think about ten people would show up."

"From both schools combined," Caitlin agreed with a laugh.

"Well, then, we have to do something that everyone will take part in," Marla said.

"Like a dance," Elizabeth suggested.

Marla pounced on the idea. "That's it!" she exclaimed, her green eyes sparkling. "A joint SVH–Palisades High dance."

Marla's enthusiasm was contagious. "Then we could each write features about each other's schools," Elizabeth said.

"We could come up with a motif and make it a theme party," Caitlin added.

"Maybe we should have a rap theme," Enid joked, turning mock-innocent eyes to Elizabeth. "Do you think we could borrow some of Jessica's music?"

Elizabeth wasn't amused. "Enid, I'm warning you," she said.

"Go, Ken, go!" Jessica yelled, her heart pounding in her chest. There was one minute left on the clock, and the Gladiators were behind by six points. The Sweet Valley High fans were on their feet screaming. Ken had the ball and he was dodging his opponents. He got in position for a pass.

"Touchdown, touchdown, touchdown!" the crowd screamed, pounding their feet on the bleachers. The stands were shaking, and the stadium was crackling with excitement.

Suddenly the Palisades linebacker blocked Ken and gave him a hit to the middle. The ball flew out of his hand and Ken doubled over, clutching his stomach. The ball bounced away and the linebacker dived for it. He scooped it up and started to run downfield.

Jessica sucked in her breath and ran as close to the edge of the field as possible. She couldn't really tell, but it looked as if the Puma had kneed Ken in the stomach. Ken was bent over, struggling for breath. He seemed to be injured. Jessica fought the impulse to run out onto the field and help him. *Why are they still playing?* she wondered anxiously. She considered running for the coach and making him call a time-out. But suddenly Ken sprang into action, lunging after the linebacker and swiping at the ball.

"C'mon, Ken," Jessica urged. The Sweet Valley fans were silent as the tension mounted.

"Ten, nine, eight, seven . . ." The Palisades fans counted down the last seconds on the clock as Ken wildly tried to recover the ball. The clock struck zero. The Palisades Pumas had won.

"Darnit!" Jessica swore, stamping her foot on the ground in frustration. The cheerleaders dropped their pom-poms to the ground and slumped onto the bench, staring at the scoreboard in disappointment.

"Here's my number," Elizabeth told Marla, scribbling her phone number on the back of a napkin as the Palisades fans leaped to their feet.

"Thanks," Marla said, wedging her shoulders free from the screaming fans to take the outstretched slip of paper.

While the players had been sweating on the field, the girls had worked out the details of the dance. They had decided to make the event a fund-raiser. They would have a friendly competition between the schools: Whichever school sold more tickets could give all the proceeds to the charity of its choice.

Balancing a notebook on her knee, Caitlin copied down her and Marla's phone numbers. "Why don't we get together on Sunday to make plans for the dance?" Caitlin suggested as she handed the slip of paper to Enid.

"We could have brunch," Enid said.

"How about the Box Tree Cafe?" Elizabeth suggested. "They do a great breakfast buffet, and there's a beautiful view of the ocean."

"I think you talked us into it," Marla laughed.

Suddenly the girls were caught in a shuffle of people pushing down the aisle.

"What's all the commotion about?" Caitlin asked.

Elizabeth looked up at the scoreboard. "Oh, I guess the game's over," she said. "I wonder who won."

Chapter 2

Ken violently slammed his locker shut. He was getting dressed with the rest of the guys from the team. Usually the locker room was like a zoo after a game, but today the atmosphere was quiet and subdued. The Gladiators' spirits were low.

Ken couldn't believe they had lost. And it was all his fault. He had totally blown the last pass. Ken replayed the moment in his head as he toweled off his hair and threw on a T-shirt. He could feel the rough leather of the ball in his hand, and he could hear the fans shouting. He saw his wide receiver, Danny Porter, in position near the end zone. The coast was clear. He lifted his arm for the winning throw . . . and suddenly a shooting pain stabbed him in the stomach. Someone had knocked the wind out of him. He gasped for air and fumbled the ball.

Ken gritted his teeth thinking about it. The

Palisades linebacker, Greg McMullen, had deliberately kneed him in the stomach. And then, to make matters worse, Greg had taunted him. "What's wrong, windbag?" Greg had snickered. "Ball too slippery for you?"

Ken could only wheeze in retort. Why hadn't he said something back? Ken threw his gym bag onto the bench in disgust.

Tim Nelson, the defensive linebacker, walked into the locker room, a towel wrapped around his waist. "Good game," he said, clapping Ken on the shoulder.

Ken grunted and sat down on the bench, fumbling under it for his shoes. He pulled them out by the shoestrings and pulled on a black high-top sneaker, a scowl spread across his face.

"Hey, don't worry about it, man," said Tad "Blubber" Johnson, his ample stomach creasing in rolls as he leaned over to put on his socks. "They were hitting below the belt."

"You can say that again," Danny said angrily, pulling on a pair of jeans. "They were out for blood."

Robbie Hendricks threw his clothes into his locker with a vengeance. "They took Bryce and Ricky out in the first half."

Zack Johnson, the linebacker, slammed his fist against the locker so hard that the entire row reverberated. "I'd like to take all of *them* out," he said, his eyes glinting angrily.

Ken sighed. Ricky's knee was damaged and

Bryce had a concussion. Bryce would be OK, but he wasn't sure about Ricky. Knee damage was a serious problem for athletes. It was possible that Ricky would be out for the rest of the season. And Ricky was indispensable to the team. Ken clenched his jaw angrily. He'd seen teams play dirty before, but never as low as the Pumas had played that day.

"I don't think we should take this sitting down," Zack said, leaning against a row of lockers.

"Too bad we don't have another game coming up," Danny added, tossing his uniform into his gym bag. "Then we could give them a taste of their own medicine."

"Who says we need a game?" Zack asked.

Zack's right, Ken thought. He wasn't going to let the Pumas abuse his players and get away with it. The Gladiators could get their revenge off the football field. Ken opened his mouth to agree with Zack, but then he stopped himself. He was the captain of the football team. It was his job to set a high standard for the morale and ethics of the team.

Ken stood up and faced the rest of the guys on the bench. "Look, guys, we're all-star quality this year. We've got an exceptional team," he said. "Our record is clean. We don't want to stoop to their level. We don't need to engage in foul play to win."

"But they're going to sabotage our chance for the title this year," Robbie protested.

"We can't just let them get away with it," Danny added.

21

Ken held up a hand. "We played our best, and more important, we played fair. And that's what counts. Remember, the old saying is right: It's not winning or losing, but how you play the game." Ken slung his gym bag over his shoulder and turned to leave. "See you at practice on Monday."

"See you," the guys mumbled, sounding discouraged.

We played our best, Ken repeated to himself as he walked out of the locker room. *And that's what counts*. If only he could really believe his own words.

"Ken!" Jessica called excitedly as he exited the locker room. Ken turned to see Jessica running to him, her face glowing. She looked beautiful, as always. She was wearing white jeans and a light-blue cotton button-down shirt, and her golden hair was falling in soft waves around her face. Her blue-green eyes sparkled and her smile shone brightly. Usually just the sight of Jessica raised Ken's spirits, but now he was too depressed even to manage a smile.

Jessica flung her arms around his neck. "How's my star quarterback?" she asked. She leaned her face back for a kiss.

"Hi, Jess," he said, giving her a perfunctory kiss on the lips and shrugging off her arms. He felt irritated by Jessica's high spirits. He wasn't in the mood for her perkiness.

"I can't believe we lost!" Jessica burst out. "It was so close."

"Yeah, and it was my fault," Ken mumbled.

Jessica wrapped an arm around his waist. "Of course it wasn't your fault, silly," she said. "You played a great game. You made two touchdowns."

Suddenly a car horn blared.

"Hey, lovebirds!" Amy yelled, waving out the window of Lila Fowler's lime-green Triumph.

Lila rolled down her window. "You guys coming?" she asked. "The whole gang's going to the Dairi Burger." The Dairi Burger was the most popular teenage hangout in Sweet Valley.

"One sec," Jessica called, holding up an index finger. She hooked her arm into Ken's. "Let's go. They're waiting for us."

But Ken shook his head. "I don't think I'm up to it."

"C'mon," Jessica said in a cajoling tone, giving him a charming smile that caused the dimple in her left cheek to deepen. "It'll help get your mind off the game. You can have your favorite strawberry shake." Jessica lowered her voice to a whisper. "And then a late-night drive to Miller's Point—"

But Ken cut her off, shaking loose her arm. "Jessica, I said I didn't want to go," he said sharply—more sharply than he'd intended.

Jessica looked wounded for a minute, then shrugged. "Fine with me," she said curtly. "See you."

She skipped off to Lila's car without a backward glance.

"Jess . . ." Ken called after her halfheartedly. But she was already hopping into the car. He stood and watched as Lila revved the engine and screeched out of the parking lot.

"Ahh, the sweet taste of freedom," Todd said as he backed his black BMW out of his space in the parking lot at Sweet Valley High. He wiggled the toes of his left foot as he pressed down on the gas pedal. It was so good to be able to move both of his feet again. He felt as if he'd been in a cast forever.

Todd cruised the parking lot, looking for Ken or Elizabeth. He'd arrived at halftime, but the stands had been so crowded that he hadn't been able to find anyone. He'd ended up taking a seat on the highest tier of the bleachers and had been barely able to make out the action of the game. The Sweet Valley High fans had spent most of their time on their feet screaming, and some girls in front of him had been holding a huge banner.

Todd decided to take a quick spin down the highway while he was waiting. Elizabeth and Ken would probably be a while. It would take some time for the stands to empty out, and Ken had to change out of his football uniform—and probably had to boost the morale of his team, as well. From what Todd had gathered from the fans around him, the Palisades Pumas had played a brutal game.

Todd swung onto the main road and pushed hard on the accelerator, enjoying the sensation of the asphalt racing beneath the wheels of his BMW. He opened the window, letting the cool night air whip through his curly brown hair. He felt as if he'd been rejuvenated. He was itching to start working out again. He was going to train like a madman in order to get back into shape.

Todd took the ramp onto the highway and cut across the road to the left lane. He raced down the smooth road, his spirits high. *My life has been like a roller coaster lately,* he thought, shaking his head. Just last week he had felt as though nothing was going his way. He had damaged his ankle during the most important game of the season. All the college representatives had been there, and Todd had been determined to make a good impression. Instead, he had come down hard on his foot and had seriously hurt his ankle. The coach had thought he would be out for the season.

Then Elizabeth had taken a trip to SVU to visit her brother and had decided to stay there for good. When she had broken the news to him, Todd had been devastated. He had felt as if his whole life were falling apart. Everything that mattered to him was slipping out of his fingers—first basketball, then his girlfriend.

But now things are looking up, Todd thought happily, taking the exit ramp and swinging back onto the main road toward the high school. He'd be back on the court in no time, and Elizabeth had decided to stay in Sweet Valley. The doctor had been very pleased with his progress. He'd said Todd's ankle had healed perfectly and that he could start practicing in a week.

Todd slowed down and turned into the Sweet Valley High parking lot, which was now packed. Some kids were piling into cars and hopping onto motorcycles, and others were hanging around, talking in animated groups. Todd weaved his way carefully through the crowded lot, looking for familiar faces.

"Hey, Wilkins!" a voice yelled from behind him. Todd pulled the car to a stop and leaned out the window. Aaron Dallas jogged over.

"Need a lift?" Todd asked, leaning over to open the passenger door.

"Thanks, man," Aaron said. He climbed into the BMW. "My car's in the shop, and I lost the guys in the crowd on the way out."

"Have you seen Elizabeth around?" Todd asked.

Aaron shook his head. "I haven't seen any of the girls at all tonight."

"Well, maybe I'll catch her at the Dairi Burger," Todd said, revving the engine. "That's where you're headed, right?"

Aaron smiled. "Where else?"

Todd put his foot on the gas gently, slowly making his way through the parking lot.

"That was a close game, wasn't it?" he asked.

"I just made it in time for the second half."

"You missed quite a show," Aaron said. "The Pumas pulled just about every stunt in the book."

Todd shook his head. "Those guys give sports a bad name."

"Hey, there's Ken," Aaron said, pointing across the lot.

Todd looked in the direction he indicated. Ken was standing alone at the far end of the parking lot. He was walking in a small circle, mumbling to himself and kicking at the gravel.

"Uh-oh, looks like some male bonding is in order," Todd said.

Aaron nodded. "Big time," he agreed.

Ken kicked at a stone aggressively. The guys on the team were dissatisfied with his decision to turn the other cheek, and now Jessica was mad at him as well. He wasn't sure if he should have given the guys his pep talk. As captain of the football team, he was the one responsible for the well-being of the squad. It was his role to keep the ethical standards of the team high, but it was also his role to protect his players from foul play. How could he just let those Palisades punks take his players down one after another?

Suddenly Todd's BMW roared to a stop by his side.

"You coming to the Dairi Burger?" Todd asked, leaning out the window.

"Nah, I'm gonna just hang low tonight," Ken mumbled.

Todd cut the engine, pulled open the door, and sprang out of the car. "Look, man!" he exclaimed, jumping from one foot to the other.

Ken didn't know why Todd was doing a dance on the pavement, but it was irritating him. Everybody seemed to be in a good mood except for him. First Jessica. Now Todd. Didn't they realize the football team had just been slaughtered and that he had been personally humiliated?

"Notice anything different?" Todd asked.

Ken sniffed the air. "Are you wearing a new perfume?" he asked sarcastically.

Todd rolled his eyes and lifted a foot in the air.

"Oh, you got your cast off," Ken said in a lackluster voice. "That's great."

Todd looked at Aaron and shook his head. "It's worse than I thought." Aaron climbed out of the car and stood next to Ken.

"What's worse than you thought?" Ken asked.

"The postgame blues," Todd said. "I know it well."

Aaron clapped Ken on the shoulder. "Hey, don't take it so hard," he said encouragingly.

"From what I could see, you guys looked great out there," Todd said. "We should have won."

"That's just it," Ken said. "They took out my best players deliberately in the first half of the game."

"I heard about it," Todd said. "The ref should have done something about it."

"He couldn't," Ken said. "The Pumas were sneaky—and smart. Only the players could tell their hits were illegal. From the stands it looked like everything was in order."

Aaron shook his head. "Maybe the ref couldn't do anything, but it was clear to everybody what was going on. Players don't go down that hard in a normal football game."

"That's right," Ken said, clenching his jaw angrily. "And I don't like to see my players being abused that way."

"Let it go," Todd advised. "They may have won the game, but we're going to win the season."

Suddenly heavy footsteps sounded behind them on the gravel. "Well, if it isn't the little windbag!" a voice said behind Ken's back.

Ken wheeled around. It was Greg McMullen, the Palisades linebacker. Even without his football pads, he was a hulking guy. Two burly dark-haired friends flanked him.

"What did you call me?" Ken asked, his eyes flashing.

"I called you the little windbag," Greg said in a jeering tone. He turned to his friend and made wheezing noises, imitating the sounds Ken had made after he had got the wind knocked out of him. The guys snickered.

Ken could feel his blood boiling. His whole body tensed, and he clenched his fists into tight balls at his sides. He rocked on his feet, ready to lunge at Greg.

Todd blocked Ken's way with an arm. "Ignore them," he said in a low voice. "They're all talk and no action."

"What did you say?" Greg asked, his tone menacing.

"Nothing," Todd muttered, taking Ken's arm and trying to lead him away. Ken shrugged him off angrily.

"You want to say that to my face?" Greg taunted.

"Yeah," Ken said, taking a few steps forward and facing him squarely. He could feel the blood pounding through his veins, and he was itching for a fight. "He said you're all talk, McMullen."

Greg's eyes narrowed dangerously. "We'll see about that," he hissed. He jumped forward and punched Ken in the stomach, knocking the wind out of him again. Ken stumbled to the ground, gasping for air. The guys snorted, pretending to huff and puff. As the pain throbbed in his stomach, Ken was suffused with rage. He leaped to his feet and flew at Greg, his face contorted in pain. Todd jumped forward and grabbed Ken, locking him in a wrestler's hold.

"Let me at him!" Ken growled, struggling with Todd to break loose and lashing out with his fists. He felt like a caged animal struggling to get free.

"Aaron, help me out here!" Todd called. Aaron rushed over and pinned Ken's arms to his sides. Ken kicked at them both with his feet.

"C'mon, Ken," Todd said between clenched teeth. "Get in the car."

Aaron pulled open the door of the passenger seat, and the two of them finally managed to push Ken in.

Greg and his friends snorted with laughter.

"What's wrong?" Greg jeered. "Afraid Matthews will break a fingernail?"

"Good thing you've got your little friends to protect you," his friend sneered.

Todd started the engine and peeled out of the parking lot.

Ken slammed his fist into the dashboard as Todd swung the car onto the main road. Then he fell back against the seat, seething in frustration. He would find a way to get back at those Palisades jerks. This time they had gone too far.

Chapter 3

"Hey, you girls wanna join us?" a guy with curly blond hair yelled at the beach on Saturday afternoon.

"We could use a little diversity," his friend said. He was a big guy with shaggy brown hair and a dark tan, and he was holding a vollcyball in his hand.

Jessica smiled at the guys flirtatiously, enjoying the attention. She was with Lila and Amy at Ocean Bay, the most popular beach at Sweet Valley. They had been cruising the beach for the past hour, checking out guys and showing off their bathing suits. Jessica was wearing a new red string bikini, and Amy had on a floral pink two-piece. Lila was sporting the latest fashion her mother had brought back from Paris, a white maillot with a sash around the waist.

Amy pushed her sunglasses on top of her head. "They're kind of cute," she whispered.

Jessica looked over the guys at the net. She wouldn't mind playing some volleyball. But the guys on the team were all unattractive and looked as if they belonged in a science lab, not on the beach.

"Amy, maybe you should put your glasses back on," Jessica said. "Look at the rest of the team."

"Jessica, sometimes you can be such a snob," Lila said, putting a hand on her hip and striking a pose for the benefit of the two guys.

Jessica snorted. "Coming from you, that's a compliment."

The curly-haired guy swaggered up to them. "Well, you up for it?" he pressed.

"No, thanks," Lila said. "We want to go where the action is."

"We'll give you action," his friend said in an insinuating tone.

"Not that kind," Jessica retorted. "And definitely not from you."

The girls sauntered off down the beach, laughing.

Jessica shook out her golden-blond hair, enjoying the feel of the sunlight pouring down on her back. It was a perfect day for the beach. The sky was a robin's-egg blue, and the sun was shining down brightly on the sparkling aquamarine water. *Actually,* Jessica reflected, *any day in Sweet Valley is a perfect day for the beach.* But today was special. It was the annual all-day surfing competition. This year there were cameras from Rock TV, the music-video channel, taping the entire event.

34

"Let's go back to the main boardwalk," Jessica suggested. "I want to check out the surfing contest." Actually, Jessica was less interested in the surfing competition than in the live cameras. She wanted to be an actress, and she had a recurring fantasy of being discovered by a famous director and becoming an overnight sensation. She didn't like to pass up any chance to get on TV.

"Sure you do," Amy teased. "I think you want to check out the surfers."

"Who, me?" Jessica said innocently. "I have a boyfriend."

Lila laughed. "That's never stopped you before."

"Look who's talking," Jessica retorted.

Weaving their way through the hordes of young people dotting the beach, they made their way back to the main boardwalk. It appeared as if the entire population of young people in Sweet Valley had turned out for the surfing event.

"Looks like the girls' competition is over," Amy said as they joined the crowd in the sand. A bunch of young women in wet suits were standing by the cameras. There were only guys out in the water riding the waves. They were practicing for their competition later that afternoon.

Jessica dropped her beach bag onto the sand and fished through it. She had forgotten to bring her towel. "Lila, did you bring something to lie out on?" she asked.

"Of course," Lila said. "I always sun in style."

She pulled a folded-up wine-colored Persian rug out of her bag and threw it onto the ground. Jessica picked it up and flung it across the sand. A gust of wind caught it and sent it flapping wildly in the air.

"Jes-si-ca!" Lila yelled as bits of sand flew into her face. She ducked and jumped out of the way.

"Oh, sorry," Jessica said. Amy grabbed a corner of the rug, and they laid it flat on the ground. They quickly jumped on to anchor it.

"Sometimes you can be so annoying," Lila told Jessica, kneeling down on the rug and running a finger through her tangled hair.

"Oh, c'mon, Lila, it's just sand," Jessica said. "We lie on it all the time."

"I like to walk on the sand," Lila corrected her. "I don't like to bathe in it." Lila stood up and shook out her hair, showering Jessica with tiny grains.

"Lila, that's not funny!" Jessica protested, wiping off the rug with the back of her hand.

Lila plopped down onto the rug, turning an innocent face to Jessica. "What? It's just *sand*."

Jessica grinned in spite of herself. She pulled out a lime-flavored Perrier. "Here, drink this and shut up," she said, handing it to Lila.

Lila laughed. "Thanks," she said, unscrewing the cap and taking a big gulp.

Jessica turned her attention to the surfers in the ocean. "Wow, they're really pros," she said.

"Yeah, they're amazing," Amy agreed.

Jessica watched in awe as the boys practiced their moves in the high-rolling breakers of the foamy Pacific Ocean. They were definitely experts. Each one seemed to outmaneuver the others. One guy was standing on his head on a surfboard, riding the wave upside down. Another had two boards and was stepping from one to the other. A guy on his right was spinning on the tail of his board in a perfect three-sixty.

"Look, a tandem surf!" Amy said, pointing out to sea. A guy in a brightly colored orange wet suit was riding a cresting wave, the nose of his surfboard pointing to the sky. A terrified-looking cocker spaniel was sitting on the edge. Suddenly a huge wave appeared on the tail of the first one and overtook it. The dog and rider flew into the water. Moments later the dog's nose popped up and he swam, panting, toward shore. Trotting out of the water happily, he shook his body violently, spraying the girls with water.

"Gross!" Lila shrieked, flicking away a speck of water from her arm. "A canine!"

Amy knelt on her towel and hit her leg. "C'mere, boy!" she called, but the dog ran down the beach.

Jessica stood up and wiped wet sand off her legs. "Let's get closer to the camera," she suggested. "Maybe we can get interviewed."

Lila snorted and pushed her sunglasses up

on her forehead. "For what? Looking good?"

Jessica shrugged. "You never know."

The girls made their way across the warm sand and joined the crowd near the camera. The winner of the girls' surfing competition was being interviewed—a tough-looking girl named Rosie Shaw. Her short reddish-blond hair was wet, and she was wearing dark sunglasses. Her surfboard was propped in the sand by her side.

Jessica looked on with envy as the girl played up to the camera. All Jessica needed was one short interview. If she could just get a few minutes on television, some well-known director would be sure to notice her.

"Will you look at that?" Lila asked as they watched Rosie being interviewed. "That is the tackiest bathing suit I have ever seen." Rosie was wearing a fluorescent lime-green bikini with neon-pink straps.

"It's hideous," Amy agreed.

"Jessica, can you believe it?" Lila said.

"No, I can't," Jessica said. But she wasn't referring to Rosie. She had just spotted an incredibly gorgeous guy. He was out in the ocean, riding a ten-foot swell. The other surfers had dived through the wave and were floating on their boards, but he was standing above them all. Poised on the white summit with his feet buried in the churning foam, he looked like a Greek god, like Mercury on winged feet. Even from where she was, Jessica could tell he had a body like sculpted marble.

"And Wilkins takes the floor!" Todd said, picking up a grapefruit and pretending to bounce it on the ground. "He dribbles down the center of the court, pivots to the left, and drives to the middle. The fans are going wild! Wilkins gets in position, leaps up, and . . . slam dunk! Two points!"

Elizabeth rolled her eyes as Todd clowned around in the grass. It was Saturday afternoon, and she and Todd were having a picnic at Secca Lake. It was a beautiful day. The sun was shining brightly, and the lake was a clear, sparkling blue. Elizabeth had gone all out, preparing an elaborate spread of salmon, arugula salad, fruit, cheese, and French bread. And to top it off, she had brought homemade brownies and sparkling apple cider.

Elizabeth tore a piece of bread off a baguette and coated it lavishly with warm Brie cheese. She stuffed it into her mouth, feeling dissatisfied. Todd didn't seem to be sharing her mood. Ever since he had picked her up, he had talked nonstop about getting his cast off. Elizabeth didn't know what was worse—when Todd had his cast on and talked about getting it off, or when he had it off and talked about nothing but basketball.

Elizabeth brushed the crumbs from her lap and stood up. "Todd, do you think you could take your mind off basketball for one moment to take part in our picnic?"

But Todd ignored her. "The forward has the ball!" he said, running toward Elizabeth and circling her, his hands held out as if he were blocking her. "Wilkins is guarding her. She's young. She's blond. She's beautiful." He jumped from side to side in front of her, making her feel dizzy.

"Todd!" Elizabeth protested, trying to get out of his way.

"She tries to dribble past him, but—" Todd leaped onto the blanket and dived for Elizabeth, tackling her to the ground. "He bumps her to the floor! It's a foul for Wilkins! Free shot for the beautiful forward." Todd smothered her face in tiny kisses.

"Your shot, Liz," Todd whispered.

Elizabeth fended him off, but she couldn't help laughing. "Todd, sometimes you can be so idiotic."

"That's just because I'm so happy," Todd said, picking up his plate and taking a bite of salad. "Last week I was a wrecked man. My girlfriend was leaving me, and I was out for the season. Now I've got the two most important things in the world back again: basketball and my girlfriend."

Elizabeth feigned hurt. "You mean I'm only as important as basketball?"

Todd paused, pretending to be deep in thought. "Hmm, which is more important?"

"Todd, that's not funny," Elizabeth said, picking up her champagne flute and taking a sip of apple cider.

Todd nodded solemnly. "You're right, basketball is obviously more important."

Elizabeth whacked him in the arm, sending his fork flying out of his hand.

Todd put his plate down and his expression turned serious. "Liz, you know you're the most important thing in the world to me." He turned and looked at her, his coffee-colored eyes warm with love. Elizabeth's stomach fluttered at the intensity of his gaze.

"Liz, it's so nice to have you back again," Todd said in a husky voice, taking the glass out of her hand and setting it down. "For good." He took her in his arms and kissed her deeply. Elizabeth closed her eyes and returned the embrace with ardor, wrapping her arms around his neck. But in the middle of the kiss Todd suddenly pulled away.

"Todd, what is it?" Elizabeth asked.

"For a second I thought that was Greg McMullen, the Palisades linebacker from the game last night," Todd said, his expression grim. Todd was staring at a couple that had spread out a blanket near them. He sighed. "But it just looks like him."

Elizabeth shrugged, rolling her eyes. Football and basketball. That's all she seemed to hear about lately. Wasn't there anything else in the world besides sports?

41

Elizabeth quickly changed the subject. "Todd, I met some girls from Palisades last night at the game," she said, excited to tell him about their plan for the dance. "We came up with a great idea." But then she noticed that he wasn't listening. "Todd?"

"I'm sorry, what?" Todd asked.

Elizabeth sighed and fell back onto the blanket, dropping a grape into her mouth. It looked as if they were going to have to talk about sports. "What's wrong?" she asked.

Todd shrugged. "Oh, nothing, really. Ken just had a little run-in with Greg McMullen after the game yesterday."

Elizabeth sat up again. Now she was interested. "What do you mean, a run-in? Did they get into a fight?"

"Well, not really. Actually, Greg socked Ken in the stomach. And then Ken tried to fight back. But Aaron and I broke it up."

"Well, that's good," Elizabeth said with relief.

Todd shook his head. "I don't know. It was a bad scene. I've never seen Ken like that. He was sort of . . ." Todd paused, searching for the right word. "Possessed," he said finally. "I've never seen Ken act so violent."

"I can't believe it," Elizabeth said, shaking her head. "Ken is normally so gentle."

"I know," Todd said. "I don't know what got into him."

"Well, at least nothing happened," Elizabeth said.

Todd shook his head. "Not yet, anyway." He had a worried expression on his face. "I don't think Ken is going to take this lying down. This isn't the last we're going to hear of Greg McMullen."

Elizabeth stared out at the still blue lake. Even though the sun was shining brightly, a chill traveled slowly up her spine.

Todd turned to her. "I'm sorry, what were you saying? You met some girls at the game?"

Elizabeth bit her lip and waved a dismissive hand. "Oh, it was nothing," she said. Now was not the time to mention her plans for the dance.

"Attention, all surfers!" a voice squawked over the loudspeaker at the beach.

Jessica opened her eyes and flipped to her side to see what was going on. She was lying out on the Persian rug with Lila and Amy, listening to rock music from Amy's portable CD player. Rosie Shaw was sitting on a towel next to them, talking to two guys. She had really been irritating Jessica. Every male of the species that had passed by had stopped to congratulate her. She'd been asked out by at least five guys in the last half hour.

The hip host of Rock TV was standing with a microphone in the middle of the beach in front of the cameras. She was wearing a funky tube miniskirt and a spandex half top. "Rock TV is sponsoring a statewide surf contest in one month!" the host announced.

Lila yawned and picked up her suntan oil, pouring a handful into her hand.

"There will be two winners, one male and one female," the host continued. "Not only will our two winners get an exclusive interview on RTV, but they'll also get an all-expenses-paid surfing trip to . . . Hawaii!"

"Did you hear that?" Jessica asked, sitting up. This was the chance she had been waiting for. If Jessica could get an interview on RTV, she would be sure to be discovered.

"Uh-oh," Amy said to Lila. "Jessica has that look in her eyes."

"I'm going to win that interview," Jessica declared. "And the trip to Hawaii."

"Oh, rad, man, I'm really psyched," Lila said, making fun of surfing jargon.

"Cool out, a surfing competition," Amy chimed in. "That's really gnarly, dude." Rosie turned toward the girls and gave them a dirty look.

"Surfing is a serious sport," Jessica said. "It developed in Hawaii in the eighteenth century."

Lila looked at her in surprise. "How do you know that?"

Jessica shrugged. "I know more about surfing than you think."

Lila scoffed as she rubbed oil onto her legs. "Well, you may know something about surfing,

44

Jessica, but that's not going to help you win the contest."

"Why not?" Jessica demanded.

Lila laughed. "Because you don't know how to surf."

Jessica shrugged. "So I'll learn."

Lila snorted. "In a month?"

"Sure, I'll pick it up with no problem," Jessica said. "After all, I've been cheerleading for years. The principle is the same. It's all about coordination and balance."

Amy looked at her in shock. "Jessica, have you forgotten all your disastrous attempts in the past?"

Jessica crossed her arms over her chest. "Like what?" she asked.

"Like, for example, the time you tried to ride a ten-foot wave and almost drowned," Amy pointed out. "You had to be fished out of the water by two lifeguards. And then you had to be revived by mouth-to-mouth resuscitation."

"Oh, that," Jessica said. "Well, what do you expect? That was my first time out. I was in way over my head."

Lila laughed. "You can say that again."

"Hmmph," Jessica pouted.

"How about when you 'borrowed' Steven's surfboard and lost it in the waves?" Lila added, snickering.

"That was an accident," Jessica explained.

Amy giggled. "Or the time you took a surfboard out in the water but you were too scared to stand

45

up, so you lay on the board all day and fried your entire body."

Lila laughed. "You looked like a boiled lobster."

Jessica's face flushed pink. "I didn't feel like surfing that day. I felt like tanning."

"Toasting is more like it," Amy corrected.

"Jessica, give it up," Lila advised. "There's no way you could win that contest." She snickered. "In fact, I bet you couldn't even stand up on a surfboard."

Jessica set her jaw and turned to Lila. "Would you like to put your money where your mouth is?"

Lila nodded. "Sure. What do you have in mind?"

"If I don't come in first place in the surfing competition, I'll wear a fluorescent-green wet suit to school for an entire day."

Lila laughed, a smug expression on her face. "You've got a deal. And if you win that contest, I'll wear hot-pink oxide on my nose for a day."

"One order of fries and three diet sodas, please," Jessica said, placing her order at the concession stand. As she waited, she daydreamed about her trip to Hawaii. She saw herself out in the ocean riding huge cresting waves, surrounded by a group of good-looking Hawaiian surfers. She pictured herself sitting under an umbrella on the beach, drinking an exotic Hawaiian shake through a long colored straw. She imagined herself dancing at a nightclub, wearing a grass skirt and a flowered lei.

46

Jessica snapped out of her reverie as the guy behind the counter handed over her food.

"Thanks," she said, opening her straw beach carry-all and placing the paper bag inside. As she ruffled through her wallet for money, she heard a whisper behind her.

"She's the one I was telling you about," said a girl's voice.

Her friend giggled. "Oh, the *cheerleader*," she mocked.

Jessica threw her money down and whirled around. It was Rosie Shaw. A tall, muscular girl in a bright-blue wet suit was standing by her side. "What's so funny?" Jessica demanded.

"You are," Rosie said.

"What are you talking about?" Jessica asked menacingly, stepping away from the counter and putting her hands on her hips.

"Two large mango fruit juices, please," Rosie said to the guy behind the counter.

Rosie turned toward Jessica. "You think surfing is a sport you can pick up in a month?"

"Surfing isn't as easy as it looks," her friend added.

"I never said it was easy," Jessica said hotly. "I'm planning to practice intensely."

"Girls like you can't surf," Rosie scoffed. "All you can do is lie on a beach and look good." She gave the guy behind the counter a dazzling smile as she took her drinks and moved away from the concession stand.

Jessica's mouth dropped open. "How would you know?" she demanded, outraged.

"Because I just happened to overhear your conversation," Rosie said, a haughty expression on her face. "You don't know anything about surfing. Surfing is *nothing* like cheerleading." She laughed arrogantly. "Surfing is a real sport. You don't just jump up and down waving pom-poms in the air and yelling 'rah rah.'"

Jessica could feel her blood boiling. She gritted her teeth and looked at Rosie through narrowed eyes. "*You* don't know anything about cheerleading."

"Well, I know one thing," Rosie replied in a condescending tone. "Pom-pom girls stand on the sidelines cheering the athletes on. Surfers *are* athletes."

Jessica bristled at the term "pom-pom girls." "Cheerleading is a sport just like surfing," she said, infuriated. "In fact, it's an art form."

Rosie burst out laughing and Jessica's face flamed. How dare this total stranger insult her? And call her a "pom-pom girl"? Who did she think she was to make fun of cheerleading? Jessica clenched her hands into tight fists at her sides. She wanted to wipe the smug expression off Rosie's face.

Rosie looked Jessica up and down, her syrupy voice dripping with disdain. "Well, cheerleaders practice in the afternoons. Surfers go out at five A.M. I can tell you don't have that in you. You wouldn't get your beauty sleep."

"We'll just see about that," Jessica said, her eyes

48

blazing. "I'll see you in exactly one month." She pivoted on one bare foot, then stopped and turned back. "And you'd better start practicing. Your next competition isn't going to be as easy as today's was."

Jessica could hear the girls giggle as she stormed across the beach, her face as hot as the burning sand. Now she was mad—and determined.

Chapter 4

"Pick me up at eight, OK?" Jessica said to Ken on the phone Saturday night, twirling the phone cord around her finger while wading through the clothing strewn about on her bedroom floor. As usual, the placc looked like a disaster zone, the floor piled ankle-deep with magazines, clothing, and CDs. "I want to go to the Beach Disco."

Jessica kicked up a short purple T-shirt dress and caught it in her hand, shaking out the wrinkles. She held it up to herself in front of the mirror. *Not bad*, she thought. *This might work for tonight*.

"Uh . . . um," Ken stammered.

"I've decided to give you another chance to go out with me," Jessica said, throwing the dress onto the bed. She cleared out a space on the floor with her foot and sat down on the rug. Last night on the way to the Dairi Burger, she had been furious that

Ken had blown her off. Actually, it wasn't so much that he hadn't wanted to go out with her, it was the *way* he had refused. He had acted as if she were invisible. But then Amy and Lila had cheered her up. "Give the guy a break," Amy had said.

"Yeah, his team has just been massacred," Lila had added.

Jessica had decided that her friends were right. She shouldn't take Ken's behavior personally. He was just upset about losing the game. *That's the downside of going out with the captain of the football team,* mused Jessica. *You get the glory, but you also get the pain.*

"Uh, actually, Jess, I don't think I can make it tonight," Ken said.

"Of course you can!" Jessica insisted, leaning back against the bed and putting cotton between her toes. "C'mon, Ken, you can't just lie around and mope all weekend." She fumbled around in the cosmetics scattered about on the floor and picked out a jar of pink nail polish.

"Well, that's not it, exactly," Ken said.

"What is it, then?" Jessica demanded, leaning forward and carefully applying nail polish to her toenails.

"I'm just not up for dancing tonight," Ken explained.

"You don't have to dance if you don't feel like it," Jessica countered, waving her foot in the air to dry her nails. "You can hang out at one of the tables and admire your girlfriend from afar." She, on the other hand, was raring to go dancing. She was so burned up about her encounter with Rosie on the beach that she was full of raw energy. And for Jessica, the best way to deal with anger was to work it off. Preferably on the dance floor.

"Uh, I, um . . ." Ken's voice trailed off.

Jessica stood up and crossed the floor on her heels, dragging the phone line behind her. Now Ken was beginning to make her suspicious. Why did he sound so nervous? Had he had a personality transformation overnight? "C'mon, Ken, out with it."

"Actually, some of the guys are going over to Bruce's tonight," Ken said finally.

"What for?" Jessica asked, picking up a brush from her dresser and running it through her thick blond hair.

"We thought we'd just shoot some pool and hang out in the rec room," Ken said.

Jessica stopped in midstroke, thinking for a minute. "Well, maybe I'll go to the Beach Disco with Amy and Lila, and then we'll stop by later."

Ken coughed uncomfortably. "Uh, actually, I don't think that's a good idea."

Jessica stared at the receiver in consternation. What was going on with Ken? He blew her off last night and now he was blowing her off again. "Why not?"

"Well, it's kind of a guy thing," Ken explained.

"Oh, c'mon," Jessica scoffed. "Guys never mind when girls show up."

Ken sighed audibly. "We're starting a club," he said.

"What kind of club?"

"A . . . er . . . guys' club," Ken mumbled. "Tonight's a GNO."

"A GNO?" Jessica asked.

"Guys' Night Out," Ken explained.

"That's the stupidest thing I've ever heard," Jessica said, and she slammed down the receiver.

What makes the Palisades Pentagon *one of the hottest school papers in the southern-California area? Marla Daniels, its fiery redheaded editor in chief.*

Elizabeth sat in front of her computer on Saturday night, clacking away at the keys. She was working on her "Personal Profiles" column covering Marla Daniels from Palisades High. Elizabeth quickly made an outline for the column, dividing it into three main sections—personal life, school activities, and political views. Maybe she could interview Marla at brunch the next day.

As Elizabeth typed out questions on the screen, her head swirled with possibilities for the dance they were planning. Using her mouse, she clicked open her dance file. Ever since she had talked with Marla and Caitlin at the football game, her mind had been whirling with ideas. She was thrilled to be able to devote her energy to something again.

Elizabeth's thoughts came so fast that her fingers couldn't keep up with them. She quickly typed in fragments of ideas for the dance—a fifties sock hop, a twenties flapper dance, a dance-athon, a costume ball . . . ballroom dancing? Elizabeth sat back and envisioned the scene dreamily. She pictured a huge ballroom with marble floors and a chandelier, like something out of an eighteenth-century French novel. The girls were all wearing long ball gowns and the guys were dressed in black tuxedos. They waltzed and tangoed across the floor to the delicate strains of classical music. Then she quickly deleted the words from the screen. The school gym wasn't exactly a ballroom. And none of them knew how to do ballroom dancing anyway.

Elizabeth opened a new file and labeled it "Party Ideas." She and Enid had already planned to get together the next morning to make posters and flyers. On Monday they wanted to start getting everybody hyped up for the dance. Elizabeth quickly typed out some slogans on the screen: "Party with Palisaders," "Sell Sweet Valley," "Dance the night away, for your favorite charit-ay." Elizabeth groaned. That last one was a major stretch.

Suddenly the door flew open. "You will not believe what the guys are doing now!" Jessica declared, stomping into Elizabeth's room. She was waving her brush in the air and brandishing it as if it were a weapon. "I mean, of all the idiotic ideas, of all the—" Jessica interrupted herself. "Sometimes the guys surprise even me with their stupidity."

Elizabeth looked up from her computer and sighed. "Jessica, do you know why there's a door in my room?"

"So I can come in, of course," Jessica said, flopping down onto the chaise lounge. Elizabeth had found the old chair in an antique market and had re-covered it in soft, pale velvet. Jessica laid her brush on her stomach and put her hands behind her head, dangling one bare painted foot in the air.

"So you can *knock*," Elizabeth corrected her.

"But what's the point of that?" Jessica asked. "I knew you were in here."

Elizabeth shook her head. Sometimes her sister's logic mystified her. She saved her file and turned around to face Jessica, pulling her legs onto the chair. She had learned long ago that she would get no work done when Jessica needed to talk. "So what's going on?" she asked.

"The guys are starting a boys-only club," Jessica explained. "And they're having their first meeting tonight. It's GNO."

"Girls no?" Elizabeth guessed.

"Something like that," Jessica said. "Guys' Night Out."

Elizabeth laughed.

"Liz, this isn't funny," Jessica protested. "This is social discrimination."

"Sometimes we have Girls' Night Out," Elizabeth reminded her twin.

"That's different," Jessica said.

Elizabeth raised her eyebrows. "How so?"

"Because we *need* to have Girls' Night Out. This whole world is a boys' club. Girls need to stick together. Otherwise, we just spend all our time hating each other and ourselves and competing for boys' attention." Jessica took a breath. The words had come out in a rush.

Elizabeth looked at Jessica in surprise. Usually her sister's number-one principle was competing for guys' attention. In fact, she had spent the day cruising the beach with Lila and Amy in her new string bikini. "Jessica, are you feeling OK? You're beginning to sound like a feminist."

Jessica made a face. "You're right," she said. "I'm beginning to sound like *you. Bleah!*"

Elizabeth laughed. "Actually, I agree with you in principle. It's just that I think it's pretty harmless in this case."

"Harmless!" Jessica said. "It's Saturday night, and we have no dates. You call that *harmless*?"

Now Jessica was beginning to sound like herself again. "Jess, you know you can go out with your friends tonight. Why do you need Ken?"

"Because I want to go dancing," Jessica said. "Lila is not exactly the best partner for slow dancing."

"Then you can dance fast," Elizabeth said.

"That's not the point," Jessica said. "Like you said, it's the principle of the thing."

"Actually, it's probably a good idea," Elizabeth said. "The guys can bond and make each other feel important. Then we won't have to worry about stroking their fragile male egos."

Jessica huffed. "All guys ever do is bond."

"I don't think we have to worry about it, anyway," Elizabeth said. "They'll get sick of each other pretty fast."

"Well, I'm getting sick of them," Jessica said, jumping up and sending her brush flying to the ground with a clatter. Jessica reached for it and held it in the air like the torch on the Statue of Liberty. "I'm going to bed," she announced. "I've got somewhere to be at sunrise tomorrow morning."

Elizabeth lifted an eyebrow. Jessica usually didn't make it out of bed until noon on the weekends. "You're getting up early on a Sunday?"

"Sure, why not?" Jessica asked.

Elizabeth shook her head. She would believe it when she saw it.

"Ace!" Aaron called, sinking the eight ball smoothly into the corner pocket.

"Man!" Bruce complained, throwing his cue stick onto the table.

Ken leaned against the wall, taking in the action. He was playing pool in the luxurious rec room of the Patman mansion with the rest of the guys—Todd,

Aaron, Bruce, Winston, and Ronnie Edwards.

Ken stifled a yawn as he watched Bruce set the balls up in a triangle on the green felt table. The evening seemed to be going on a bit too long. The guys had been hanging out all night. First they'd had a barbecue out on the deck. Even though the Patmans had a live-in French chef, the guys had decided to rough it. They had barbecued hamburgers and hot dogs on the grill, eating them with chips and soda on paper plates.

Afterward some of the guys had taken a swim in the Patman's heated Olympic-size pool. Ken and Todd had played a few sets of tennis in the tennis court cut into the hill below the mansion. Then they were all pretty tired, and they'd crashed in the living room. They lay around for an hour, watching rock videos on RTV. And now they were winding up the evening with a few rounds of pool.

Exactly what you'd expect from a GNO, Ken mused. Male camaraderie and male companionship. The evening had worked out perfectly. The food was good, the sports were good, the conversation was good. *Then what's missing?* Ken wondered. But he knew what was missing. *Girls*.

Ken shifted his weight as Todd and Winston practiced their shots. Todd hit the cue ball into the triangle, sending the other balls whizzing around the table. Then he leaned over the table like a pro, taking careful aim at a striped ball. It careened off a solid one, banked off the four sides of the table, and dropped smoothly into the side pocket.

"Perfect bank shot!" Todd said.

"Let me try that," Winston said. He got in position, leaning over the table and holding his cue stick awkwardly. His knobby elbows sticking out, Winston slid the stick along the table, aiming for the ball. His stick went flying over the table. Todd ducked and all the guys laughed.

"Winston, you're a liability," Todd said.

"Actually, I did that on purpose," Winston said with a goofy grin, retrieving his stick from the carpet. "I wanted to make sure you were on your toes."

Ken laughed along with the rest of the guys, but he didn't really feel in the spirit of things. The evening was actually kind of boring without any girls around. And Ken was getting tired of sitting around with the guys while they tried to amuse themselves. He would rather be with Jessica at the Beach Disco.

Ken's stomach tightened anxiously as he thought about his girlfriend. He wondered if Jessica had gone out dancing with Lila and Amy. Of course she had. Jessica wasn't one to sit around and wait for her boyfriend. In fact, she was probably having the time of her life, dancing in the arms of some other guy right that moment. And looking incredibly sexy.

What's she wearing? Ken wondered. *Is she wearing her white jeans? Who's she dancing with?* Suddenly Ken was hit with a sharp pang of jealousy. He wanted to run out to his car and drive to the Beach Disco. He would claim his girlfriend from the greasy paws of the slimy guy who was dancing with her.

It's all my fault, Ken thought with a sigh. Jessica had wanted to go out with him. But he had disappointed her last night, and he had turned her down again tonight. Jessica had been sweet and supportive after the game, and Ken had barely acknowledged her presence. He knew Jessica wouldn't accept that kind of treatment for long. He had learned his lesson when she had gone to SVU and had started dating a guy behind his back. She had believed that Ken didn't value her for her intelligence, so she had found a guy who did. Ken bit his lip. Now that he had Jessica back, he didn't want to lose her again.

Ken glanced furtively around the room. All the guys were hunched over the pool table. They had started a new round and had divided up into two teams. Maybe he could just put in a quick call to Jessica. Then he would feel better. If she was home, then he could apologize and make plans to see her the next day. And more important, he would know she wasn't gyrating on the dance floor with another guy. And if she was out, he'd leave a message. Then she wouldn't be so mad when she got in. Ken edged toward the door, trying to appear nonchalant.

The guys were involved in the pool game and didn't seem to notice as Ken slipped out the door. He sneaked down the elegant hall and picked up the phone receiver from a marble side table. He needed only a few minutes. His heart pounding in his chest, he began quickly punching in Jessica's phone number.

"Hey, Matthews, who you calling?" a gruff voice came from behind him.

Ken whirled around, facing Bruce guiltily. "Er . . . uh . . ." he stammered, hanging up the phone mid-dial.

"Matthews, you're a wuss," Bruce said. "GNO means *no girls,* in person or on the phone." Disgust was written all over his face. "Your problem is you don't have any backbone. You let women dictate your entire life. I'm telling you, you've got to learn to bond with the guys." Bruce headed back to the rec room, shaking his head the whole time.

Bruce is right, Ken thought as he followed him down the ornate hall. If he hadn't got so soft-hearted, he wouldn't have let the Palisades line-backer clobber him on the football field. Or in the parking lot after the game. Sweet Valley would have won. And he'd still have his dignity.

"Man, those Palisades guys are such jerks," Aaron was saying as Ken walked into the rec room. Aaron was sitting at the square wooden game table with Winston, dealing out cards. Ronnie was sitting in front of the Patmans' elaborate hi-fi system, flipping between radio stations with the remote control.

"I'd like to cream them all," Bruce said. He

leaned over the pool table and angrily shot a ball into the corner pocket.

"Ken, you in?" Aaron said. "We're playing poker."

"Sure, I'm in," Ken agreed, pulling up a chair.

Aaron rubbed his hands together. "OK, guys, this is five-card stud." Aaron passed out chips and dealt the cards. "Nothing wild."

Bruce picked up his cards and paced around the room. "Those guys are asking for a fight," he said.

Ken exchanged a glance with Todd, thinking about his encounter with the Palisades guys after the game. Just remembering it caused him to get all worked up again. He was still burning from his humiliation of the night before. "Yeah, I'd like to meet those guys in a dark alley," he said.

Bruce got a gleam in his eye. "What do you say we pay a visit to Palisades High?" he asked the group. "I have a few gallons of white paint. We could write a really nice message on their football field."

"I don't know if that's such a good idea," Winston said carefully. "We'd just be asking for trouble."

"That's the whole point, Egbert," Bruce said, his voice laden with disgust. "Are you scared of trouble?"

Winston didn't back down from Bruce's challenge. "I just don't know if it's wise to take this any further. The Palisades guys are obviously trying to bait us. Maybe we shouldn't rise to the challenge."

"This is a GNO, right?" Bruce said, swaggering around the room with his cards in his hand. "We're here to learn how to be real men. And real men don't take this kind of thing lying down."

"But vandalizing school property is a serious crime," Winston said.

Bruce marched across the room and stared at Winston. "And what do you call deliberately injuring players on the football field?" he challenged him. "Child's play?"

Winston didn't flinch from his stare. "That doesn't mean we have to stoop to their level," he insisted.

"I say an eye for an eye, a tooth for a tooth," Bruce said.

Winston looked around at the other guys nervously, silently pleading for help. But everybody was quiet. It was obvious that Bruce had intimidated them. None of them wanted to be the one to say it was a bad idea.

"Let's just finish this round first," Aaron said diplomatically.

"Why don't we let the cards decide?" Winston suggested.

"You got it, Egbert," Bruce said. "Winner decides."

Ken studied his hand. All he had was a pair of nines. He didn't actually know if he wanted to win or lose. He was aching to get revenge. But he also knew that Winston was right. They could get caught by the police and be taken to the station. They could be thrown into jail for the night. Or even be expelled from school. And it would only serve to provoke the guys from Palisades. The rivalry wouldn't stop there.

But then Greg McMullen's sneering face popped into Ken's mind, and his blood started boiling again. Ken was aching to vindicate his team. If they vandalized the Palisades football field, then the guys from Palisades would know they weren't dealing with wimps. They would think twice before they tried to abuse his players again. Ken wanted to win the round. He decided to bluff. "I bet a dollar," Ken said, throwing in a blue chip.

Todd threw his cards onto the table. "I'm out."

"I'll match you and raise you a quarter," Winston said, throwing in a blue chip and a red chip.

"Raise you five bucks," Bruce said, throwing in five blue chips.

Ken sighed. "I'll stay."

"Me, too," Winston said.

Bruce rubbed his hands together. "Show time!" he said.

Ken showed his hand. "Pair of nines," he said, throwing his hand on the table.

Winston laid his cards faceup on the table, looking hopeful. "Full house."

A triumphant grin spread across Bruce's face. "Royal flush," he said, turning his cards around and revealing a run of face cards and hearts. The guys looked at each other in silence.

"Let's go, men!" Bruce said, scraping back his chair and standing up purposefully. "After all," he said with a wicked grin, "it's in the cards!"

The guys grabbed their jackets and headed for the door.

As he walked through the foyer, Ken stopped and took a look in the mirror. His eyes were dark and his skin was pale. He had a bad feeling about this.

Chapter 5

Early Sunday morning Jessica steered the Jeep into the parking lot of a small, secluded, unnamed beach near the border of Sweet Valley. There was just one other car in the lot, an old powder blue Volkswagen bus, and she parked next to it. Rubbing the sleep out of her eyes, Jessica pulled Steven's old fiberglass surfboard out of the car. She couldn't believe she actually had managed to get up this early. Dragging herself out of bed had been more difficult than studying for a final exam in chemistry. Was she losing her mind?

A light breeze wafted through the parking lot, sending bits of sand flying into the air. Jessica blinked and shivered, wrapping her arms around her body. It was chilly early in the morning, and she was wearing only a terry-cloth cover-up over her bathing suit. Jessica hesitated before making her way down the beach. A picture of her warm, cozy bed flashed into her mind. Maybe she should just turn around and go back home. She could curl up under the rumpled covers and sleep until noon, then shuffle into the kitchen and make pancakes for breakfast. And nobody would be the wiser.

Except Lila and Amy. They would be thrilled to hear that she had given up surfing before she had even begun. She could just picture the smug expression on Lila's face as she said, "I told you so," in an annoyingly singsong voice. There was nothing worse than hearing Lila say "I told you so." Jessica felt like kicking herself. Why had she told them she wanted to learn to surf in the first place?

Because of Rock TV and the trip to Hawaii, that was why. She had a chance to get on television and win a paid vacation to Hawaii. Of course she could learn to surf. After all, she was the cocaptain of the cheerleading squad. All it took was a little coordination and skill. And a lot of courage. Jessica bristled as she thought of Lila's taunt from the day before: "I bet you can't even stand up on a surfboard." And Rosie Shaw's words came back to her: "All you can do is lie on the beach and look good."

Jessica's face set with determination. She was going to learn to surf and make Lila and Rosie eat their words.

Jessica strode purposefully across the beach and dropped her bag onto the damp sand. Pulling a fluffy blue beach towel from her bag, she shook it out and spread it on the ground. Then she stripped down to her new racing suit, a maillot with purple and yellow stripes. Jessica wrapped her arms around her body as she took in the surroundings. The beach was deserted and the horizon was a dull blue-gray. The ocean looked cold and unwelcoming, a vast green tumult of angry breakers and frothing whitecaps.

Grabbing the surfboard, Jessica walked quickly down the beach. She shivered as she waded into the sea. The water was icy cold. She should have borrowed a wet suit. Then she looked out across the ocean and shivered again, this time from fear. The waves were larger than she had expected, and she didn't see any other surfers.

Jessica stood at the water's edge, contemplating the movement of the ocean. She hadn't ever really thought about it before, but the waves seemed to have a life of their own. It was as if they were battling one another. Rising to roaring peaks, they came down in angry explosions of white foam. As one wave surged up the beach, the next followed right on its tail. The waves were coming in sets of threes, and the final surge always won. Each billow was higher than the last, building up to a crescendo until the third wave reached its churning pinnacle and crashed down in a mighty white avalanche of churning foam.

Jessica took a deep breath and gathered together her courage. *There's only one way to learn,* she thought, paddling with the board through the breakers. *Besides*, she reassured herself, *the waves always look bigger from the shore*. She went out farther and farther, not wanting to admit to herself she was scared. As she reached the lifeguard buoy indicating deep water, she stopped and took a rest. Draping her arms over the board, she let herself be lifted with the rise and fall of the waves.

Finally she called on her Wakefield spirit and decided to stand. A small wave was approaching. Jessica lay on the board, setting herself up behind the breaking lip. As the wave caught her board, she straightened to her full length. The wave threw her off balance, and she went flying backward into the water, her surfboard darting away. Breathing heavily, she surfaced and recovered her surfboard. As the next wave rolled in, she climbed up on the board and tried again. The wave rushed in to meet her, carrying her up in the air and sending her diving forward into the water. Undaunted, she repeated the effort several times. But each attempt had the same result: She was scarcely upright before she found herself flipping into the water.

Then Jessica saw a huge wave coming. It was rushing toward her in a rising white crest, building up momentum as it rolled through the stormy ocean. *This is it,* Jessica thought, steeling herself. *Time to sink or swim.* Her heart pounding like a jackhammer in her chest, she lay on the board and waited for the wave to reach her. She began to paddle hard and turned to meet the powerful curling wave.

As the wave caught the tail of her board, she sprang quickly to her feet. The wave scooped her up and carried her with it. Adrenaline shot through her veins. She was riding high on the surging crest, skimming the surface of the ocean. It felt like flying. Salt water whizzed by her, and cool wind whipped through her hair. Jessica could see for miles.

But as soon as the sensation began, it was over. The water came up to meet her, and the surfboard shot out from under her feet. Jessica was sucked into a pressure-filled vortex, crushed under mountains of cascading white water. She tumbled and turned, whirling about in a salty green chaos. She gasped for breath and swallowed mouthfuls of salt water. Rocks and sand crashed into her face; salt water went up her nose; something slimy wrapped itself around her thigh.

Finally the wave deposited her near the ocean's edge. Coughing and sputtering, she knelt and gasped for breath. Her eyes were hot and searing, and her lungs burned. Her entire body felt sore and bruised. She shook her hair out and pulled the seaweed off her leg. She scanned the water for her board but couldn't see it anywhere. It was gone.

Exhausted, Jessica made her way to the beach. She flopped down onto her towel, pounding the sand with her fists in frustration. At this rate, she would never learn to surf. After all her efforts, she couldn't even manage to stand up on a wave for more then two minutes. And now she didn't even have a surfboard. Jessica stretched her arms over her head and closed her eyes, letting the early-morning sun lull her to sleep.

A few minutes later Jessica awoke, feeling the sun blocked from her body. She lifted her head to see her surfboard standing in the sand. She followed it up and met a lithe, muscular form and a pair of smoky blue eyes.

"Looking for this?" the guy asked in a husky voice.

"Ahh . . . fresh-roasted coffee and a view of the sea," Marla said happily. She took a sip of her cappuccino.

"The perfect Sunday morning," Caitlin chimed in.

Elizabeth smiled, pleased with her choice of restaurant. She and Enid were having brunch with Marla and Caitlin at the Box Tree Cafe. They were sitting at a table outside on the terrace overlooking the ocean. The cafe was known for its buffet-style Sunday brunch. An elaborate spread was set out on a long table covered with an elegant white tablecloth. They had their choice of fresh bagels, smoked salmon, scrambled eggs, a variety of cheeses, croissants, and fresh fruit. They had all loaded up their plates and were drinking coffee and fresh-squeezed orange juice.

"The view is exquisite from here," Caitlin said.

"It is, isn't it?" Elizabeth agreed, gazing out at the breathtaking seascape. The ocean was a bright sparkling blue-green with frothy white combers. Buoys bobbed up and down on the horizon, and a sailboat was floating lazily in the waves. The ocean was dotted with windsurfers wearing brightly colored wet suits and swimmers frolicking in the shallow water. From Elizabeth's vantage point up on the terrace, they looked like colorful specks in the water.

"Let's get down to business," Marla said. She put down her coffee and picked up a spiral notebook. "If we don't start now, we're going to eat ourselves into a coma."

Elizabeth laughed. The girls had been chatting for the past half hour, getting to know each other and swapping stories. She'd been having such a good time that she had almost forgotten about the dance.

Caitlin leaned over to look in the notebook. "First of all, we need to come up with a theme," she said.

"I was thinking about it yesterday," Elizabeth said. "What do you think about a fifties sock hop?"

"I don't know," Caitlin said, taking a sip of coffee. "I like the twenties better."

"That's not a bad idea," Marla put in. "We could have a swing dance with jazz music." She picked up a buttery croissant.

Elizabeth sliced a bagel and covered it with cream cheese, adding a thick slice of smoked salmon. "The only problem is that we'd need a swing band," she said. "I was thinking of asking The Droids to play at the party. They're a really big rock band at our school." She paused for a moment, considering. "Of course, we could just have a disc jockey and play CDs."

"No, you're right. I veto my idea," Marla said, breaking off a flaky piece of her croissant. "Live music would be much better."

"Maybe we should have a costume party," Enid proposed. She lifted a forkful of scrambled eggs to her mouth.

"I know!" Marla said excitedly. "We can have a masked ball."

"That's perfect!" Caitlin breathed. "That way both schools will be dressed in disguise, and we'll be forced to mix with each other."

Marla fished a pen out of her bag and scribbled the theme down in her book.

"Great," Elizabeth said. "Now we just need to find a place to hold the dance."

"How about Ocean Bay?" Enid suggested. "We could do some kind of barbecue and have a beach party."

"I think we'd need to get a license for that," Elizabeth said. "After all, it would be a huge party with both schools there."

Marla lifted a strawberry to her lips and smiled. "Actually, Caitlin and I have found a perfect spot."

"You have?" Elizabeth exclaimed. "You Palisaders sure work fast."

"It's an old warehouse located midway between the towns, so it's neutral territory," Caitlin explained. She reached for the cheese plate in the middle of the table and cut off a wedge of Camembert.

"And best of all, we can rent it dirt cheap," Marla said. "It's about to be made into a dance club, so the owner isn't worried about it getting damaged."

"I think that sounds amazing," Enid said. She turned to Elizabeth. "What do you think?"

"I agree," Elizabeth said, her blue-green eyes sparkling brightly in the midmorning sun. It looked as if they were really going to pull this off. "With a few weeks of work, we should be able to get the place all fixed up for the dance."

"Well, there's just one problem," Caitlin said. Enid and Elizabeth looked at her expectantly.

"The renovation on the warehouse starts in eight days," Caitlin explained.

"Eight days!" Enid exclaimed. "That means we'd have to have the dance Friday night."

Marla nodded ruefully. "It'll be a record breaker in terms of quick planning," she said.

"I don't know," Enid said worriedly. "That only gives us four days to get ready. Do you think it's possible?"

"Of course it is," Elizabeth said, rising to the challenge. Actually, she was glad to have a tight deadline. She'd been needing a project like this to get her juices flowing.

*　　　*　　　*

"The most important thing is to ride down the face of the breaking wave," Christian said to Jessica as they walked down the beach carrying their surfboards.

"OK." Jessica nodded, smiling at the gorgeous guy next to her. She couldn't believe her luck. Out of all the beaches, in all this world, this incredible guy had walked onto hers. His name was Christian Gorman. He had wavy dark-brown hair and smoky blue-gray eyes, and he looked as if he had grown up in the sun. He was wearing a red-and-gray wet suit and he was tanned a smooth golden brown. His eyes crinkled when he talked, as if he were always squinting into the sunshine.

They walked into the ocean and waded through the gentle rolling breakers at the shoreline. When they were waist-deep in water, Christian lay down flat on the board on his stomach, demonstrating the proper method for paddling. Placing her surfboard flat on the water, Jessica followed his example.

As they paddled out to deeper water, Christian gave Jessica a number of tips. "Remember the golden rule of surfing—don't fight the surf, go with it," he instructed. "A surfing master once said that the best a surfer can ever hope to do is harmonize with the wave; he can never master it."

"Maybe that's why I couldn't get up before," Jessica said, musing aloud. "I was thinking of the ocean as a raging battlefield."

"Well, maybe it is," Christian said. "But then

you've got to join the front. You can't fight it."

When they reached deeper water, Christian demonstrated how to get up on the board. "Actually, the most difficult part of surfing is learning to stand up," he said. "Once you've got that down, it's smooth sailing." He hopped up onto his board, riding low with his knees bent and his arms outstretched. Then he came off the lip and paddled back to her.

"The classic California style of surfing is noseriding," Christian explained as he reached her. "You paddle as the wave approaches and lift the nose of the board till the wave catches it. Remember, you don't ride the wave. It rides you."

Jessica nodded. What Christian was saying made sense. Now she understood why she had had so much trouble standing up earlier. She had been trying to jump onto the wave. It was only when she had let the wave carry her that she had managed to ride for that one exhilarating moment.

"Jessica, I think that wave is calling your name," Christian said as a modest swell approached. "Just try to stand," he encouraged her. "Let the wave take you."

Wanting to impress him, Jessica concentrated and followed his instructions exactly. She pointed the nose of the board down the line, hopping up as the wave caught her. "Keep your knees bent at all times," he said, touching her leg lightly. A thrill chased up Jessica's spine at his touch. Holding her arms outstretched, she managed to maintain her stance for a few seconds. Then she felt her balance slipping. She slid off the board onto her stomach and paddled back to Christian.

"Great!" Christian encouraged her. "You were able to stand." A large wave approached and Christian turned around, positioning the tail of his board in the direction of the lip and beginning to paddle. "Now, watch my technique," he said. Jessica floated on her board and looked on in awe as Christian let the blue comber sweep him up, then followed the crest of it. He rode with an ease that made surfing look as natural as walking.

"Remember, follow the face of the wave," he shouted over the pounding surf. He shifted his body and cut a smooth zigzag pattern across the surface of the water. "You steer the board by shifting the weight of your body."

A steep wave followed quickly on the heels of the last one. Jessica dived through it and watched as Christian followed it to its peak, flipping the board in the air and landing with bent knees on his surfboard. He rode over the back of the wave and slid onto his stomach in one clean motion. Then he paddled toward her with strong, smooth strokes.

"That was just to show off," he said, giving Jessica a rakish grin. "I don't usually have beautiful girls for an audience this early on Sunday morning."

Jessica's face flushed. "Well, I'm impressed," she admitted.

"OK, now let's try it together," Christian said. A large wave was rolling toward them and gaining momentum.

"Get in position," Christian instructed.

Jessica lay on her board, her whole body tensed.

"Ready? Now!" Christian called.

Jessica began to paddle as hard as she could. As the wave lifted her, she sprang to her feet. She shifted her weight and let the wave carry her, using the muscles in her legs to maintain her balance. Suddenly she was soaring across the ocean. It felt as though she were riding a moving mountain of water.

"Look, Christian, I'm up!" she screamed. He had also caught the wave and was close beside her. "I'm—" Suddenly the wave overtook her.

"Christian!" Jessica cried, grabbing on to him for support. They both tumbled into the water. Laughing, they caught hold of their surfboards and shook the water out of their hair.

"I told you I'm a beginner," Jessica said as they paddled back to the beach. She was out of breath, but her aquamarine eyes were bright and sparkling.

"You're doing great," Christian encouraged her. "You'll be doing three-sixties in no time."

"Only if I have a teacher like you," Jessica said as they waded out of the water and gathered their belongings. Jessica rubbed herself dry and pulled on her white cotton swimsuit cover-up.

"I'll tell you what," Christian said. "I'll agree to

give you surfing lessons if you'll agree to take them."

Jessica laughed at his logic. "You drive a hard bargain, Christian Gorman," she teased.

"So what do you say?" Christian asked.

"You've got a deal," Jessica said, holding out a hand.

Christian shook her hand and held it a moment too long, looking at her with liquid fire in his eyes. Jessica's heart flip-flopped. She pulled her hand from his quickly, turning away and picking up her bag.

As she and Christian walked up the beach to the parking lot, Jessica suddenly remembered her boyfriend. Ken wasn't going to be thrilled about the lessons. But, then, that was his problem. He was the one who'd been ignoring her lately.

Christian threw her surfboard into the Jeep, and Jessica hopped into the driver's seat.

"Since tomorrow is a school day, we'll have to meet earlier," Christian said. "I'll see you at five o'clock." He gave her a wink and sauntered away.

Jessica gulped. *Five o'clock? On a Monday?*

But then she looked at the beautiful, sculpted muscles of Christian's back as he walked away. And she remembered how great her one second on that wave had felt.

Jessica shrugged as she backed out of the parking lot. She'd manage.

"Want some more?" Ken asked on Sunday night, offering Jessica a spoonful of Raspberry Twirl yogurt.

"Umm," Jessica said, taking a bite. They were sitting side by side on the edge of the Wakefields' in-ground swimming pool, dangling their feet in the cool blue water.

Ken took Jessica's hand in his, feeling calmer in her presence. It was quiet and peaceful by the pool. The white pavement was surrounded by crisp green hedges and flowering rosebushes. The air was light and balmy, with just a slight scent of roses. The wooden deck near the kitchen added a faint pine scent to the air.

As they sat by the side of the pool, Ken could feel his fury about the game dissipating in the cool night air. His anger had somewhat abated after the boys' late-night escapade at the Palisades football field. They had scaled the fence surrounding the field and painted a huge message in thick white letters on the green turf. The message was Bruce's idea—"Palisades Pumas Purr Like Kittens."

Afterward they had hopped over the fence and had run as fast as their legs could carry them to their cars. Ken knew it was a stupid idea to vandalize school property, but he had needed an outlet for his aggression. He felt better afterward. He was glad he had let the Palisades guys know they couldn't mess around with his players. But now the rivalry seemed far away, and even a little silly. He had made his peace with it.

Now he just had to make things better with Jessica. Ken had arrived at the Wakefields' unexpectedly that evening, wanting to surprise her. He had brought a gallon of her favorite frozen yogurt as a token of his affection. He knew he had to show how much he appreciated her.

He had interrupted the Wakefields' dinner and had sat down to eat with them. Jessica hadn't seemed thrilled to see him. Her demeanor had been cool and distant. "Oh, hi, Ken," she had said. "C'mon in." She hadn't even kissed him hello. It was as if he were only a friend of the family. And she had been oddly quiet and distracted all through dinner. She barely spoke at all. She was probably still mad that he had blown her off twice in a row.

"So what did you do last night?" Ken asked, feeling somewhat nervous about her response. He knew how stubborn Jessica could be. He had to make an effort with her if he didn't want to lose her. If Jessica had been mad at him and alone at the Beach Disco with her friends, anything could've happened.

A mischievous grin crossed her face. "Just went out with the girls," she said lightly. "We all trekked out to the woods and made a witches' brew. With rats' tails and spiders' legs. You know, Girls' Night Out."

"Jessica, c'mon," Ken protested.

"And then we made voodoo dolls and pulled their legs out," Jessica added, giggling. "Did you feel any pain?"

"No, but I think you're pulling my leg now," Ken said.

Jessica smiled. "So how was your GNO?"

"Actually, it wasn't too much fun," Ken admitted. "It got kind of boring just hanging out with the guys." He turned to her and put his arms around her. "I missed you," Ken said in a throaty voice, leaning in to kiss her. Jessica gave him a quick kiss and pulled out of his arms abruptly. She turned away and picked up the carton of yogurt.

"Actually, we went on a manhunt," Jessica said in a teasing voice. She took a huge spoonful of yogurt and put it in her mouth.

"That's what I was afraid of," Ken said. "At the Beach Disco?"

"No, in the woods, silly," Jessica said. "We were hunting for savages taking part in ancient male bonding rituals."

Ken rolled his eyes. "Jessica, what did you do last night? You're torturing me."

"Oh, Ken, I didn't do anything," Jessica said. "I painted my toenails and went to bed." She held up her pink-tipped feet in the air. Then she looked again. Only one foot was painted. "Or at least some of them."

Ken breathed a sigh of relief. He picked up her hand and gazed into her blue-green eyes, trying to make a connection with her. But her eyes were unfathomable, like bottomless pools. "Jessica, I'm sorry I couldn't go out last night," he said.

Jessica shrugged and turned away, licking the last remnants of yogurt off the spoon. "No big deal," she said. Then she stared into the pool, seeming to study the play of light on the water.

Ken couldn't figure Jessica out. She was quiet and pensive during dinner. And now she was cool and flippant. No matter what he tried, he couldn't seem to reach her. It was as if her mind were a million miles away.

Ken looked at her profile, trying to guess her thoughts. Her high cheekbones were tinted pink from the sun, and her hair was wound down the back of her neck in a golden-blond French braid. In the soft blue light of the swimming pool, she looked like some pagan sea goddess. Ken's breath caught in his throat. "Jess, what are you thinking?" he asked.

"I think I learned what being on the top of the world means," Jessica said quietly.

"I learned what being on the bottom was," Ken responded. "On the bottom of Greg McMullen."

"C'mon, Ken, forget about that," Jessica said. "It's just football."

"Just football?" Ken protested. "That's like saying it's just air."

Suddenly Jessica looked at her watch. "Nine o'clock already!" she exclaimed. "I've got to get a good night's sleep tonight." Jessica gave Ken a kiss on the forehead. "See you at school tomorrow," she said brightly. Then she jumped up and skipped inside.

Ken looked after her, bewildered. Jessica never

went to bed early. And she never stayed in on a Saturday night. *Women*, thought Ken. *I'll never figure them out.* Then another thought struck him. She had said she knew what it felt like to be on top of the world. What had she meant by that?

Ken sighed and rested his elbows along the white pavement, his feet turning to prunes in the water.

Chapter 6

"Hey, Enid, can you hand me some tape?" Elizabeth asked on Monday morning before school. She was standing on a chair, hanging a poster on the wall over the lockers. Elizabeth and Enid had spent the last hour decorating the school with dance posters and handing out flyers advertising the event. They had made a dozen posters on Sunday with different slogans on them: "Sell Sweet Valley," "Party with Palisaders," and "Cha-cha for Charity." The flyers were black and cut in the shape of masks. "Come to the Joint SVH-PH Masked Ball" was written in gold marker along the edges.

"Coming up," Enid said, ripping a couple pieces of masking tape off the roll and handing them to Elizabeth.

Elizabeth fixed the poster to the wall. Then she jumped down, stepping back to take a look at it.

Pastel-colored paper masks cut out of tissue paper covered the fuchsia board. The masks fluttered in the air, creating the effect of butterflies flying in the wind.

"Well, that was the last one," Elizabeth said, wiping off her hands in satisfaction. Suddenly a crush of students came down the hall, and Elizabeth scrambled out of the way. She was glad they had got to school early to put up the posters. Now the halls were packed. The walls of the corridor reverberated with the sounds of banging lockers and chattering students eagerly catching up on the weekend's gossip.

"Here, have a flyer," Enid said, distributing the sheets of paper to a group of freshmen girls hanging out near the water fountain.

"Thanks," a blond girl said, looking at the paper black mask curiously.

"Cool, a dance," said a girl with frizzy brown hair and cat-shaped glasses. "We could use something to do around here."

"Liz! There you are!" Todd called, coming down the hall with Bruce. "I've been looking all over for you. I wanted to give you a ride to school this morning, but you were already gone."

Elizabeth grinned. "Enid and I had some work to do."

"Yeah, we noticed," Todd said. He had a worried look on his face.

"Party with Palisaders," Bruce sneered, reading a poster hanging above the lockers.

"Oh, c'mon, Bruce, get in the spirit of things," Elizabeth said, handing him a flyer.

Bruce muttered aloud as he read the paper. "A joint dance . . . warehouse . . . support your favorite charity . . ." As Bruce skimmed the contents, a scowl spread across his face. "I can't believe you're planning a gathering with Palisades High," he growled. "Don't you know that school is the enemy?"

"That's ridiculous," Elizabeth said. "Just because they beat us in a football game doesn't make them our archrivals."

"That's what you think," Bruce said. He crumpled up the flyer in a ball and tossed it into a trash can across the hall.

Elizabeth's mouth dropped open. "Just because you're not interested in the dance doesn't mean other students aren't," she said angrily, folding her arms across her chest.

"You'd be better off if I threw all your stupid flyers away," Bruce said. "Elizabeth, I'm warning you now, you're asking for trouble." He turned and strode away.

Elizabeth turned an outraged face toward Todd. "Can you believe the nerve of him?"

"Actually, Liz, I think Bruce might have a point," he said. "This dance may not be such a good idea."

Elizabeth threw her hands up in the air. "Both of you! I can't believe it," she exclaimed. "You guys are blowing this rivalry thing way out of proportion."

Todd lowered his voice. "You know what happened at the game," he said. "And I told you about the scene with Ken afterward."

"Oh, Todd, I think your little boys' club is getting to you," Elizabeth scoffed. "Just because you guys feel like turning a minor scuffle into a major war doesn't mean the rest of the students want to join in. Your rivalry has nothing to do with the whole student body. We'd rather have a dance. Right, Enid?"

Enid nodded her head in agreement.

Elizabeth shook her head, disgusted. "Sometimes guys think they're the center of the universe."

But Todd didn't budge from his position. "Liz, I still think this dance idea is a mistake. You should probably stop it now before it's too late," he said softly. "I just wish you'd talked to me about this first."

Elizabeth raised her eyebrows. "If you hadn't been busy with your Guys' Night Out, I would've told you all about it. But believe it or not, we women actually know how to make plans on our own."

Todd sighed. "Fine, have it your way," he said. "I'll see you later."

Elizabeth turned to Enid as Todd walked away, and shook her head. "They're out of control," she said.

"Don't worry, Liz," Enid said. "The guys are just overreacting. The dance is going to be great."

"And we're going to make sure of it." Elizabeth

ripped off a piece of tape and hung a flyer on the locker, feeling more determined than ever to hold the dance. The success of their party would prove that women know best.

"Let's skip homeroom," Jessica murmured, drifting contentedly in the lulling waves of the calm ocean. She and Christian were floating on their surfboards, holding hands. They were all alone in the sea, and it was like their own private aquatic paradise. Reflecting off the blue of the water, the light spray of the surf took on the semblance of crystal. The water particles sparkled in the sun like diamond droplets.

"Let's skip the whole day," Christian suggested.

"I wish we could," Jessica replied longingly. She'd been having such a wonderful time with Christian in the ocean that she didn't ever want to leave. The waves had been small and constant, and Jessica and Christian had been surfing all morning. At this point Jessica could stand up on her board with no problem, and she was beginning to feel comfortable with the rhythm of surfing. It was so tempting to spend the whole day with Christian. Then she could really improve her surfing. And she and Christian could lie out on the beach all day together.

But then Jessica rejected the possibility. She didn't want anyone to know about her latest activity. Lila and Amy were the only people who knew about her newfound interest in surfing, and no one at all knew about Christian. Jessica wanted to keep it that way. It would look suspicious if she didn't show up at school. Ken would ask her where she'd been.

A wave of guilt washed over her as she thought of her boyfriend. She'd been consciously pushing thoughts of Ken away all morning. Every time she pictured his warm blue eyes, she felt a pang. She had meant to tell him about her surfing lessons yesterday, but he hadn't even seemed to hear her when she'd brought up the subject. And now that she and Christian were in the ocean holding hands, she felt glad she hadn't mentioned anything to Ken.

Jessica shook away her thoughts and did a flutter kick, sending their surfboards rotating in a slow circle.

"Have you been surfing long?" Jessica asked, turning her face toward him.

"As long as I can remember," Christian said. "I was like a fish as a child."

"Me, too," Jessica said. "I've always loved the water."

"Actually, I didn't start to surf seriously until I was in high school," Christian said. He looked thoughtful for a moment. "I think it was something I needed to do."

"Why?" Jessica asked.

"Sometimes I have to find an outlet for my energy, a physical outlet," Christian explained. "I can't spend all my time sitting at a desk studying. I guess surfing is sort of an escape from my real responsibilities. It's when I'm most in tune with myself."

"I know exactly what you mean," Jessica said. "That's how I feel about cheerleading."

"You're a cheerleader?" Christian asked, looking impressed.

Jessica nodded.

"I bet you're the captain of the squad," Christian said.

Jessica made a face. "Cocaptain," she said.

Christian laughed.

"It's the most important thing in the world to me," Jessica said. "A lot of people don't understand it. My twin sister, for example."

"There are two of you?" Christian asked.

"Well, in appearance only," Jessica said. "We're completely different in character. Elizabeth is much more serious than I am. She thinks cheerleading is a ridiculous waste of time."

"That's what my older brother, Jason, says about surfing," Christian said. "According to him, surfing is just a vain activity for tanned beach bums."

Jessica looked at him, feeling intrigued. It seemed as if they had a lot in common. "What's your brother like?" she asked.

"Jason? I would say he's perfect—the perfect son, the perfect student, and the perfect friend," Christian said. "He always does everything right. He's student class president, he's editor of the yearbook—"

"He's involved in lots of extracurricular activities, he loves reading and writing, and he gets straight-A's," Jessica finished for him.

Christian looked at her in astonishment. "How did you know that?" he asked.

"Because Elizabeth is exactly the same way," Jessica explained. "She always does everything right, and I'm always getting in trouble. Sometimes I feel as if I'm the evil twin."

Christian was nodding his head as she spoke. "I know the feeling. I've always been the wild one in the family," he said. "Jason's the responsible son, and I'm the black sheep. No matter what I do, I can't live up to him."

"Maybe we should introduce Jason to Elizabeth," Jessica suggested with a laugh.

Christian shook his head. "Nah, Jason's got a steady girlfriend. They've been going out for*ever*."

Jessica laughed. "Liz has a longtime boyfriend, too."

"Of course," Christian said with a smile.

Jessica opened her mouth to question Christian further about his family, but then she changed her mind. Somehow she felt that she knew all she wanted to know about him. She let go of his hand and paddled lightly, riding over a small wave on her stomach.

"The ocean is nice today," Jessica said as she paddled back to him. "It's not like a raging battlefield. It's more like a peaceful bath."

"Yesterday was rougher than usual. The sea tends to be pretty calm early in the morning," Christian said. "These are the best waves to learn on. You can ride for a long time without getting tired, and you can really get a feel for the basic motion of surfing."

"It's beginning to feel natural to me," Jessica said.

"Jessica, you were born to surf," Christian said. "I've never seen anyone make such fast progress." He pulled himself up to a sitting position.

Jessica beamed inwardly, but smiled modestly. "That's just because you're my teacher," she said. There was some truth to her statement. She knew she wouldn't have made so much progress without Christian to inspire her. Somehow he made her feel like a different person. Her life at Sweet Valley High seemed light-years away.

Jessica sat up on her board and looked straight into Christian's face. "It's strange, but I feel like I've known you forever," she said.

"I know what you mean," Christian said, his voice husky. His smiled at her with smoldering blue eyes. "But, actually, we know almost nothing about each other."

"I'd like to keep it that way," Jessica said. "If we exist for each other only at the ocean, then we can pretend the rest of the world doesn't exist."

"That's fine by me," Christian said. "Here, with you, I can be the person I want to be. Instead of the person I am."

Then he pulled her toward him suddenly and gave her a heart-stopping kiss. Jessica knew she should be worrying about Ken at that moment, but all she could think of was Christian. And all she could feel was the sensation of his wet, salty lips on hers.

"The posters look great," Olivia Davidson said to Enid and Elizabeth at lunch in the cafeteria on Monday. "I love what you did with the tissue paper."

"Coming from you, Liv, that's really flattering," Elizabeth said, reaching for a salt shaker and sprinkling it over her platter of steamed vegetables. Olivia was the arts editor of *The Oracle* and one of Elizabeth's good friends. She was a talented painter and was known for her unconventional style of dressing.

"The flyers are awesome, too," Winston said. He picked up his grilled-cheese sandwich and took a big bite.

"Yeah, it was a really good idea to make them in the shape of masks," put in Maria Santelli, Winston's girlfriend. "Now nobody will forget to come dressed in disguise."

Elizabeth lifted a forkful of vegetables to her mouth, thrilled with all the attention. They had definitely succeeded in creating news. All anyone had been talking about all day was the dance with Palisades. It appeared that everybody was impatient for a little activity. At least five people had stopped her in the hall with ideas for which charity they should support.

Winston picked up a mask and held it to his face. "What am I?" he said.

"A masked bandit," Enid guessed. She speared a pickle with her fork and lifted it to her mouth. Winston shook his head.

"The Red Baron," Olivia suggested.

"No, no," Winston said, shaking his head again. "Maria, tell them."

"He's Batman," Maria said, reaching over to Winston's plate and grabbing a few french fries. "He wants us to come to the dance dressed as Batman and Robin."

Winston's eyes lit up. "What do you think?" he asked the group.

Maria dipped her fries into ketchup and rolled her eyes. "He thinks it's the most original idea ever."

Winston leaned into the table and spoke in a confidential tone to the group. "She's just jealous that she didn't come up with the idea first," he explained. "She actually wanted to come disguised as Batman herself."

"Winston! This is a masked ball. We're supposed to look elegant. There is no way I am coming to the dance dressed as Batman or Robin," Maria said, stuffing the fries into her mouth.

"What do you want to come as?" Olivia asked her.

"I was thinking of Marie Antoinette," Maria

said. "Then Winston could come as Louis the Sixteenth, the Sun King."

"I have an idea," Winston said. "We'll come as Batman and Marie Antoinette."

Maria pursed her lips. "Winston, if you keep this up, I'm not going to go with you at all. Then you'll have to go as the Lone Ranger."

Winston looked wounded and everybody laughed.

"So have you put together a dance committee?" Olivia asked.

Enid nodded. "We're working on the party with two girls from Palisades High."

"They're really great," Elizabeth said, picking up a fresh roll from her tray and buttering it. "Their names are Marla and Caitlin, and they're on the staff of the Palisades newspaper. We met them at the game on Friday night." Elizabeth mopped up her plate with the bread and took a bite.

Olivia whistled under her breath. "You guys really move fast," she said. "Is everything worked out?"

Elizabeth nodded her head. "Everything's pretty much in order," she said. "We're going to sell tickets out of the *Oracle* office all week and set up at the warehouse on Friday before the dance. The only thing up in the air is which charity to support."

"I've heard about a hundred different ideas today," Enid said. "The Sweet Valley Community Center, the Institute for Medical Research at Sweet Valley University, Help for the Homeless . . ."

Elizabeth took over. "The Southern California

Foundation for Abused Women and Children, Environmental Alert, Project Youth . . ." She turned to the group. "What do you think?"

Olivia shook her head. "It's almost impossible to decide. Each one is a worthy cause. How can you say one charity is more important than another?"

"Why don't you have a drawing?" Winston suggested. "We can put the ticket stubs in two boxes, one for each school. Then the king of the dance can pick out a ticket from the winning school's box and let the winning ticket holder decide."

"Winston, you're brilliant," Elizabeth said.

Winston smiled. "They don't call me Egbert for nothing."

"And who's going to be the king of the dance, I wonder?" Maria asked, turning laughing brown eyes to Winston.

"*Moi*, of course," Winston said, bowing slightly to Maria. "My queen."

Just then Lila and Amy passed by holding trays.

"Oh, Elizabeth and Enid, we're in for Friday night," Amy said, stopping by the table.

"Great, I'm glad you're coming," Elizabeth said. "You can buy tickets any time this week at the *Oracle* office."

"I think the dance is a fabulous idea," Lila said. "I've been looking for an occasion to dress up."

"Yeah, I hear Palisades is full of gorgeous guys," Amy added.

"Well, I'm glad you're into the idea, but, actually,

good-looking guys isn't our objective," Elizabeth said. "The point of the party is to bring the two schools together, and to raise money—"

But suddenly a loud chanting interrupted their conversation.

"Pain for Palisades! Pain for Palisades!"

Elizabeth twisted around in her seat and followed the sound. The commotion was coming from Bruce's table in the middle of the cafeteria. All the guys were chanting and pounding their fists on the table—including Ken and Todd. Elizabeth couldn't believe those two were going along with it. She had never known they were such sheep. She shook her head. Ever since their GNO on Saturday night, the guys had been acting like cavemen.

Another table picked up the cry. For a moment only the din of the chanting could be heard. It was like some primitive tribal ritual. A chill raced up Elizabeth's spine, and a sudden instinctive fear seized her heart.

"Liz, are you all right?" Enid asked. "You look pale."

Elizabeth forced a laugh and shook her head hard, trying to rid it of the troubling feeling. "Sure, I'm fine," she said. "Just a little surprised to see my boyfriend acting like one of the herd."

"Do you think we should still go ahead with the dance?" Enid wondered aloud.

"Of course we should," Elizabeth said with determination. "I'm not going to let a few male egos stand in my way. The party is going to raise money for charity. I'm sure the guys will come around."

Enid looked skeptical, squinting her eyes.

"The guys are just being sore losers," Elizabeth scoffed. "Nothing's going to happen at the dance."

But despite what she said, Elizabeth's mouth went dry. An eerie premonition had come over her.

Chapter 7

"Oh, no, I'm late," Ken mumbled, looking at the wooden clock on the wall of the sunny yellow kitchen of his house on Tuesday morning. He stuffed the rest of his toast into his mouth and downed his orange juice. Grabbing his keys, he swung his backpack over his right shoulder and raced out the front door of the stately stone-faced house. He hopped down the steps of the front porch and sprinted across the lawn.

But suddenly he found himself flat on his face in the dewy lawn. Something had wrapped itself around his ankle and had sent him and his backpack flying. His hands flat on the earth, Ken raised himself from the ground, as if he were doing a push-up, and stood awkwardly. Hopping on one foot, he disentangled the white material from his left ankle, looking at it curiously. Toilet paper.

His eyes narrowing, Ken searched for the source of the damage. And he found it everywhere. His entire front yard was strewn with toilet paper. It covered the freshly cut grass, the neat hedges, and the green shrubbery in front of the house. Even the tall oaks were wrapped with long white strands. It looked as if there had been a huge snowstorm.

Ken swiped at the branches of a tree, pulling off long streamers of toilet paper. He grabbed on to the bark to climb up the tree but suddenly stepped back to look at it. A big white bow had been tied around the trunk.

"Some gift," Ken said, clenching his jaw angrily. He ripped the bow off the tree, throwing the wad of toilet paper onto the ground.

Ken stalked around in a fury, collecting the long streams of toilet paper from the yard and trees and throwing them in a huge pile in the center of the lawn. *They must have used a dozen roles of toilet paper,* Ken thought. *What a waste. Don't they know anything about conservation?*

A few minutes later Ken stepped back to survey the damage. He had managed to get all the big pieces off the lawn, but tiny bits still covered the grass like flakes of confetti. The paper had disintegrated in the dew. And streams of toilet paper still waved from the upper branches of the trees.

"I don't have time for Palisades's stupid games,"

Ken muttered in annoyance. It would take him forever to clean up the lawn. And he had to make sure everything was in order before he went to school. He didn't want his parents facing this mess when they got home from work. More important, he didn't want them to know what was going on between the two schools.

Throwing his backpack onto the lawn, Ken raced back into the house. He fumbled under the kitchen counter and pulled out a big box of large green trash bags. Running out the back door to the garage, he grabbed a rake from the wall and went back outside.

"I feel like a trash picker," Ken muttered as he scrambled around the lawn, scraping up bits of toilet paper with the rake and wiping them off into the bag. Throwing the tool aside, he shimmied up the oak trees on the front lawn and pulled the paper off the upper branches.

Half an hour later Ken had filled four garbage bags. He stopped and propped the rake on the ground like a shepherd guarding his flock. The yard was finally clean. He glanced down at his watch. He should be able to make it to school in time for first period. He would miss only homeroom.

After tossing the bags into the trash bin, Ken grabbed his backpack and ran for his car in the driveway. Then he stopped dead in his tracks. His white Toyota had been egged. Ken dropped his backpack to the ground, seething with anger. He ran to the back of the car and quickly rummaged through the trunk for an ice pick. He scraped at the windshield with all his might, but the dried egg was crusted on. He'd have to take the car to the car wash and have it cleaned professionally. Ken threw the ice pick down and slammed his fist into the car.

Then he felt something squishy under his foot. He took a step back, his anger mounting. On the driveway "Palisades Rules" was written with shaving cream. Ken looked around wildly for signs of more damage. It looked as if there was a message in the street as well. Marching down the driveway, Ken stood in front of the thick, foamy letters: GET READY FOR YOUR LAST DANCE!

Quaking with rage, Ken ran back inside the house.

The phone was ringing as he walked through the door. It was probably Greg McMullen and his little friends, calling to taunt him about their little prank. Ken yanked the phone off the wall, thrilled to be able to give them a piece of his mind.

"What do you want!" he barked into the receiver.

"Ken?" a male voice asked. It was Todd.

"Oh, Todd, I thought you were Greg McMullen." Ken held the phone to his ear and paced the hall angrily. "You will not believe what those jerks from Palisades have done now. They trashed my entire lawn and my car. And they wrote some nice little messages on the street with shaving cream."

"I know," said Todd.

"You know?" Ken asked, stopping in the hall. "What do you mean?"

"The same thing happened to me," Todd explained. "And Bruce. And Aaron. And Ronnie. And Winston."

Ken swore under his breath.

"I guess they're getting their revenge for the message we left on their football field Saturday night," Todd said.

"Yeah, it looks like they decided to write back," Ken said dryly.

"Obviously Palisades wants a fight," Todd said.

"This is not just a fight," Ken said, his mouth tightening into a grim line. "This is war."

Jessica bent her knees and held her arms out for balance, coasting along a few breakers on Tuesday morning. For the tenth time that day, she glanced down at her waterproof watch. It was seven A.M. and the ocean was deserted. Where was Christian? Jessica had been out for two hours, riding the waves alone. She sighed and cut smooth carving arcs along the gentle rollers, practicing the zigzag pattern that Christian had shown her. It looked as if he had decided to ditch her.

Jessica drifted lying facedown on her surfboard, taking a rest. Maybe she'd turn in for the day. Somehow surfing wasn't as exciting without Christian there. It was kind of lonely being out in the ocean all by herself. And she didn't have as much motivation to surf without Christian to impress.

Then she spotted a lone figure approaching on the beach. Jessica raised a hand to her forehead, shielding her eyes from the sun. It was Christian. She was tempted to ride a wave to the shore and run to meet him. But then she resisted the impulse. She had to play it somewhat cool. After all, he was the one who hadn't bothered to get out of bed on time this morning.

"Sorry I'm late," Christian said as he paddled out next to her.

He was wearing a black wet suit and he looked exhausted. His face was wan, and he had dark circles under his eyes.

"Oh, that's OK," Jessica said, waving a dismissive hand.

"Have you been making progress?" he asked.

Jessica nodded excitedly. "Look what I've learned," she said. She was anxious to show him the moves that she had mastered that morning. Jessica lay down on her board and pointed the nose toward shore, thrilled to have Christian as an audience.

Paddling as fast as she could, she picked up a medium-size wave. Jessica hopped to her feet and balanced on the board, careful to keep her knees bent and her arms outstretched. She built up speed by weaving along the wave. Then she rode up to the crest and did a sharp one-eighty turn, smacking the lip and riding back down the face of the wave. Exhilarated with her performance, she paddled back out to Christian.

"What do you think?" Jessica asked, her face flushed with excitement.

"That's great, Jessica," Christian said halfheartedly, floating on his board.

Jessica's face fell. He wasn't impressed by her new moves. In fact, he barely seemed to notice she was there. Jessica picked up a wave and surfed away from him. She didn't know what his problem was, but she didn't feel like dealing with it.

Jessica lay down on her stomach, dangling her hand in the water, and, out of the corner of her eye, watched Christian surf. It seemed as if he was trying to work off some aggression. He had a look of fierce determination on his face, and he was riding the waves in the "power" style of surfing, aggressively catching them and coasting along them with smooth, powerful moves.

Jessica's breath caught in her throat as she watched Christian carve tracks in the choppy water. The wind was whipping through his wavy brown hair, and water was sparkling on his tightly coiled muscles. It looked as if he were all alone with the forces of nature. He seemed to embody all the power of the sea.

Who is he? Jessica wondered. Who was this surfing god that had appeared from out of the sea? She didn't really know anything about him. She had no idea where he lived or where he went to school. And yet she felt as if she understood him. There was an energy and a danger emanating from him. And at the same time a strange loneliness—as if he were always misunderstood. Jessica felt as if she'd met her soul mate. For the first time in her life, she was getting to know somebody from the inside out.

And what she knew of him was enough, she decided. It was better not to have too much information. The less she knew about Christian, the more like a fantasy their relationship could be. If the romance was all just a dream, then she wasn't really having an affair with a total stranger. And she wasn't really cheating on Ken.

A big wave came up unexpectedly, sweeping her into the air and flipping her off her board. Shaking the water from her eyes, Jessica grabbed her board and hopped adeptly onto it. *You don't ride the waves, they ride you,* Jessica remembered. She readied herself to catch the next surge. Suddenly a pair of strong male arms grabbed her from behind.

"Aack!" Jessica screamed.

"It's just me," Christian said. "Did you think I was a shark?"

"I think you *are* a shark," Jessica teased.

"Since my star pupil is making such good progress, I've got a new trick to show her," Christian said. He was smiling and his blue eyes were crinkling. It looked as if Christian was his old self again.

He lifted her onto his surfboard with him and picked up her board under his arm. "Tandem surf," he explained. "Just follow the movements of my body."

Jessica closed her eyes, feeling the strong, sure movements of Christian's muscular frame as he shifted his weight and cut a clean line across the choppy waves. She leaned back against him for support, and he wrapped a strong arm around her waist. For a moment they seemed to be frozen in time, their bodies molded together in the middle of the sea.

Then he brought the surfboard to a stop and they both slid off into the cool water. Jessica's whole body tingled as he released her. Treading water, Christian handed her her board. "Now you practice," he instructed. "I'm just going to take a little siesta."

Christian grabbed the incoming surge and rode it to the beach. Jessica hopped onto her board and caught the next wave. Closing her eyes, she tried to mimic Christian's stance. She tried to feel the position of his feet and the bend of his knees.

Half an hour later Jessica had the move down pat. She was riding a wave perfectly. She couldn't believe how great it was. The tremendous force of the ocean carried her along, making her feel giddy with excitement. At this point she didn't even care about RTV or Lila or Rosie.

She just wanted to stay on top of the world.

Jessica rode the wave all the way to the beach and found herself running into Christian's arms. He picked her up and twirled her around, her wet body close against his. Suddenly they were kissing passionately, madly, as Jessica had never kissed anyone before. All she could hear was the pounding of the surf in the distance and the beating of her heart against his.

When she finally pulled away, her stomach coiled. She felt as though nothing would ever be the same again. And the feeling scared her. How could she have such strong emotions for Christian when she was supposed to be in love with Ken?

The thrill of surfing is affecting me—that's all, Jessica reassured herself. But as Christian's smoky blue eyes burned into her, she knew deep down that she'd fallen in love.

"Have the guys all lost their minds?" Elizabeth asked at the *Oracle* office on Tuesday afternoon after school. She was sitting behind a computer, writing her feature story about the dance on Friday. Olivia Davidson was sitting cross-legged on the floor in front of a layout board, arranging photographs. Penny Ayala, the editor in chief, was propped up on a stool at the drafting desk, proofing a column.

"I don't know what's happening," Olivia said.

112

She picked up a negative and held it to the light, examining it carefully.

"All everyone's been talking about all day is the egging," Penny said. "The Palisades guys trashed the guys' cars and lawns."

Elizabeth sighed. "And now the guys are plotting their revenge."

"I've never seen them get so worked up about a school rivalry," Olivia added.

Elizabeth shook her head. She never would have planned the dance if she'd known it would have such disastrous results. The guys had stormed into school together late that morning in a big group. They were all wearing jean jackets and dark sunglasses. Elizabeth wondered what they'd been doing. Todd said they were late because they'd had to clean up their lawns, but Elizabeth wasn't so sure. She had a feeling that they'd been up to some mischief themselves.

In any case, they were gearing up for something. And Elizabeth feared that something was going to take place at the dance. The guys had marched around the halls all day in a pack, exciting everybody with horror stories about Palisades High. Every time Elizabeth caught sight of them, their band seemed to have got larger. By lunchtime the group had grown to include most of the guys in the junior and senior classes. Obviously, they were slowly recruiting every male student in the school. *But for what?* Elizabeth wondered.

In the lunchroom, the guys had been conspicuously absent. Elizabeth had managed to catch Todd as he'd walked through the cafeteria with Ken. She'd pulled him aside and forced him to talk to her for a few minutes. Todd had been distracted the whole time, shuffling his feet and looking at his watch. Elizabeth had wanted him to talk the guys out of perpetuating the rivalry any further. "Just tell them to rise above it," she had urged. "Violence only leads to more violence."

But Todd had barely heard her. "Liz, I gotta run," he'd said, kissing her on the cheek. "Guys' meeting." Then he had disappeared into the outdoor eating area.

The antagonism between SVH and PH seemed to have sprung up overnight, Elizabeth mused. And it wasn't a typical school rivalry. Earlier that day Todd had given her the details of the morning's vandalism. The Palisades guys had written "Palisades is #1" on Bruce's lawn and "Palisades Rocks" on Todd's driveway. But the message on Ken's street was the worst: "Get ready for your last dance." Elizabeth shivered as she thought of it. That wasn't just simple school pride. That was a threat.

Suddenly Elizabeth experienced a sense of déjà vu; the same fear she'd felt the day before seized her stomach. She sat back for a moment, her face ashen, then closed her eyes and made a quick decision. Her instincts had been telling her something all week, and it was time for her to listen.

Elizabeth tore her story from the typewriter and ripped it up. She was going to call off the dance. It was too risky. She was sure Enid, Marla, and Caitlin would agree. They had to stop this thing before it was too late.

Chapter 8

"I'm all ears," Jessica said to Ken on Tuesday afternoon. They were sitting outside in the empty football bleachers. It was a breezy day, and the late-afternoon sun was reflecting sharply off the aluminum stands.

Ken had practically attacked Jessica after cheerleading practice. "Jessica, I need to talk," he had said. His voice had sounded urgent, and he'd had a serious look on his face. Jessica was impatient to get through their meeting. She had talked Lila into going shopping with her at the Valley Mall for a wet suit, and Lila would be picking her up in a half hour.

Ken cleared his throat, looking nervous. He turned and looked at her with warm blue eyes. "Jess, I know you're upset with me, and I want to apologize," he said softly. "I'm sorry I've been so distracted lately."

Jessica couldn't meet his gaze. She turned away quickly and pushed her sunglasses up her nose. "That's OK," she said. "I understand." *It's strange,* Jessica thought. She had been so mad last weekend that Ken had been ignoring her. And then she'd met Christian. She hadn't given a second thought to Ken's behavior since.

In fact, it was odd to be sitting with Ken at all. It seemed as if they had nothing in common now. *Maybe our relationship was always entirely superficial,* Jessica mused. Maybe it was based only on a mutual interest in sports and a shared social life. Her connection with Christian seemed so much deeper. She felt as if she belonged by his side. In the ocean.

Ken squeezed her hand appreciatively. Jessica's hand burned at his touch, and she pulled it away quickly, fumbling through her gym bag for a sweatshirt as an excuse. "It's chilly out here," Jessica said, drawing a fluffy red SVH sweatshirt out of the bag and pulling it over her head.

"My behavior has nothing to do with you," Ken explained. "It's just that those jerks from Palisades have really got to me."

Jessica sighed. Ken was still talking about the football game on Friday night. Why couldn't he get over it? Carefully, she said, "Ken, I know the guys were playing dirty at the game, but don't you think you should let it go?"

Ken sighed. "Actually, Jessica, that's not all that happened."

"Oh? What else happened?" Jessica turned to face him, trying to look interested. Usually she loved to hear school gossip, but at the moment her thoughts were elsewhere. She felt a million miles away from life at Sweet Valley High. She longed to be in the ocean, to feel the water whizzing by her and the spray of salt water in her mouth. She thought of her tandem surf with Christian earlier that morning, his strong arms locked around her waist. And she thought of the passionate kiss on the beach. . . . Jessica shook her head, trying to concentrate on what Ken was saying.

"And then I had a little encounter with McMullen and his friends after the game," Ken explained. "They started taunting me. And McMullen socked me in the stomach." Ken's eyes flashed angrily as he spoke. "I wanted to hit him back, but Todd and Aaron stopped me." Ken punched the aluminum seat. "It was so humiliating. I would have loved to have given him a right uppercut to the face."

Jessica looked at Ken with concern. He was getting more and more worked up as he talked. His jaw was set and his eyes were blazing. She had never seen him look that way before.

"And then they trashed everybody's yard this morning," Ken continued. "Me, Todd, Aaron, Ronnie, Bruce, Winston." Ken ticked off the names on his fingers. He turned to Jessica, a fierce expression on his face. "Jessica, I'm a normally peaceful guy, but there are times when a man has

119

to prove himself." Ken's mouth set in a determined line. "This may be one of those times."

"How are you planning to do that?" Jessica asked, beginning to feel concerned.

"We're going to have a showdown at the dance. Just us and the Palisades guys. At the warehouse."

Jessica looked at Ken nervously. His talk was getting her worried. It wasn't Ken's style to get involved in violent activities. She didn't know what would happen if he tried to take on the guys at the dance. Ken was an athlete, but he wasn't a fighter. Those thugs could rip him to shreds.

Jessica thought quickly. Maybe if she could talk Elizabeth into canceling the dance, the whole rivalry would fizzle out. "Ken, what if there was no dance?"

Ken laughed harshly. "That'd be even better. Then we wouldn't have to worry about the other kids getting in the way." Ken gazed into space, his eyes narrowed to slits. "Jessica, we're going to show up at that warehouse no matter what. And so are they."

Suddenly a rush of guilt hit Jessica like a tidal wave. Ken was going through a really hard time, and all she could think of was Christian and the beach. Ken trusted her. He had turned to her for support and confided in her. *I don't deserve his trust,* Jessica thought guiltily, biting her lip.

Then she made a new resolve. She would make up for her lack of support by backing her boyfriend one hundred percent. She would really be there for him in his time of need and give him all the emotional support she could.

But Ken was probably overreacting. If the rivalry was as serious as he said and the guys got into an actual fight, how bad could it be?

It wasn't as if a bunch of high-school guys could really hurt each other.

"Enid, can you get the drinks?" Elizabeth asked, pouring a bag of tortilla chips into a big wooden bowl on the counter of the Wakefield kitchen. She pointed to a couple bottles of seltzer set out on the round butcher-block table.

"Sure," Enid said, tucking the bottles under her arm. She picked up four glasses in her hands and maneuvered her way carefully into the living room.

It was Tuesday afternoon, and Elizabeth and Enid were waiting for Marla and Caitlin. Elizabeth had called everybody from the *Oracle* office and scheduled an emergency meeting. She had picked Enid up on her way home and talked over the situation with her. Enid thought they should call off the dance as well.

Setting the chips aside, Elizabeth reached for the bowl of salsa she had made and placed it on the counter in front of her. She dipped a finger into the sauce and tasted it. Something was missing. The sauce needed some zest.

Grabbing a handful of onions and a garlic clove

from the cupboard, Elizabeth hopped up onto a stool in front of the counter. She squeezed garlic into the bowl with a garlic press, her thoughts focused on the dance. After all their hard work, she hated to give it up. But she knew it was the best thing to do. After all, they could always reschedule it for later in the year. *After the boys' hormones have calmed down,* she thought wryly.

Elizabeth picked out a big red onion and sliced into it on a cutting board. Her eyes burning, she chopped the onion into fine bits and scraped it into the bowl. Fat teardrops welled out of her eyes and dropped onto the counter. Elizabeth sniffed and blinked, trying to see through her tears. Adding a few drops of Tabasco sauce, she grabbed a wooden spoon from the counter. As she stirred the sauce, she took a deep breath, trying to calm her nerves. Dealing with the boys' behavior at school all day had been harrowing.

The doorbell rang and Elizabeth jumped, dropping the spoon with a clatter. Salsa splattered across the counter. *Get a grip,* she told herself, wiping up the salsa quickly and throwing the spoon into the sink.

"I'll get it!" Enid called, making her way down the hall.

Grabbing both bowls, Elizabeth carried the food into the living room. She set the chips and salsa on the coffee table as the girls entered the room. "Hi, you guys," she said, wiping her eyes with the back of her sleeve.

Marla looked at her in concern. "Elizabeth, are you all right?" she asked.

Elizabeth smiled. "Onions," she explained, pointing at the spicy sauce.

Marla breathed a sigh of relief. "Oh, I thought you were upset about the rivalry for a minute." She took a seat on the sofa and reached for a chip.

Elizabeth shook her head. "I definitely don't feel like crying," she said. "I feel like screaming." She sat down cross-legged on the shaggy rug.

"Why, what's going on?" Caitlin asked, joining Marla on the couch.

"Some of the Palisades guys vandalized the yards of some of the SVH guys this morning," Elizabeth explained.

"They appear to have done a pretty thorough job," Enid added. "Toilet paper, egging, shaving cream, the works." She poured seltzer into glasses and passed them around. Then she took a seat in the armchair, curling her feet up underneath her.

"And since then the whole school's been in a frenzy," Elizabeth told her friends. "The guys are going around in a big group, getting everybody excited."

"It was just like that at our school yesterday, wasn't it, Caitlin?" Marla said.

Caitlin nodded. "After the SVH guys painted

the football field." She picked up her glass and took a sip of seltzer.

"What?" Elizabeth exclaimed. "I haven't heard anything about that."

"They painted a message on the football field Saturday night," Caitlin explained. "Something about the Palisades Pumas acting like kittens." She dipped a tortilla chip into the salsa and crunched into it.

"The guys were roaring mad," Marla said. "They spent hours trying to hose down the field for the game this weekend."

"I can't believe it," Elizabeth said. "How could they be so stupid as to vandalize school property? And to trespass as well?" Elizabeth was outraged. Painting a football field wasn't just a minor prank. It was a serious crime. The SVH guys were acting like hypocrites. They were all worked up about a little egging when they had gone out and committed a much bigger crime themselves. Elizabeth's eyes narrowed. Maybe this school rivalry wasn't as one-sided as it seemed.

Enid shook her head. "I guess the GNOs got to them," she said.

"GNO?" Marla asked.

"Guys' Night Out," Elizabeth explained. "The latest fad at Sweet Valley. Todd said the guys were just going to hang out at Bruce's house on Saturday night, but I guess their hormones got the better of them." Elizabeth shook her head. "They're acting like Neanderthals."

"To tell you the truth, I'm getting nervous about the whole thing," Marla confided. "I think the situation's only going to get worse. The guys seem to be plotting something for the dance."

"The same threats are going around SVH," Enid said grimly.

"I hate to say it, but I think we should call off the dance," Elizabeth said.

Marla and Caitlin nodded. "We came to the same conclusion ourselves."

Elizabeth stood up and began pacing the room. "I just can't figure it out. I've never seen the Sweet Valley guys act like this," she said. "They walked around in a tight group all day, plotting their revenge. They were all wearing jean jackets and dark sunglasses."

Marla and Caitlin exchanged nervous glances. "It was the same at our school today," Marla said.

"Except the guys were wearing black leather jackets," Caitlin added.

The girls were silent for a moment, digesting the information. "This isn't just school rivalry anymore," Enid said quietly.

"It's gang warfare," Elizabeth said.

Marla looked at the rest of them, her expression grim. "It's like we've walked into *West Side Story*."

"Jessica, looking like a surfer isn't going to help you learn to surf, you know," Lila said as they walked down the crowded corridor of the Valley

125

Mall on Tuesday afternoon. The mall was packed with late-afternoon shoppers.

"Don't you always say that clothes make the woman?" Jessica asked, dodging a woman pushing a baby carriage.

"Well, they may make a woman, but they don't make a surfer," Lila retorted. "You have to *practice* to become a surfer."

Jessica stopped in front of the directory and ran her finger down the list of shops. "Bingo," she said, stopping at the listing for Sam's Sporting Goods. "Second floor."

Jessica and Lila walked to the escalator and joined the throng of shoppers riding it.

"For your information, I've been out in the ocean every day this week at five in the morning," Jessica told Lila as they reached the second floor.

Lila snorted. "Oh, right. You can barely make it out of bed in time for school."

The girls got off the escalator and made their way through the arcade of shops. "This way," Jessica said, turning to the left and leading Lila into Sam's Sporting Goods. "It's true," she insisted. "I've got the basic motion down. And I'm already able to do a one-eighty."

"Oh, sure," Lila scoffed. "Have you got any proof of that?"

"As a matter of fact, I do," Jessica said. "I happened to meet—" But then she stopped herself midsentence. She waded through the racks of sporting-goods clothes, wondering if she should tell Lila about Christian. Even though Lila was her best friend, Jessica knew she wouldn't be able to keep such a great secret to herself. Actually, she would probably tell only Amy. But then Amy would tell Maria. And Maria would tell Winston. Eventually Ken would find out, and Jessica couldn't allow that to happen.

Besides, Jessica didn't actually feel like confiding in Lila about her new romance. Usually Jessica wanted to tell Lila everything, but this time she felt like protecting her privacy. She wanted to keep her life with Christian all to herself, like a precious secret. Jessica wrapped her arms around her chest, thinking dreamily of her morning on the beach.

"So what is it?" Lila demanded.

"What's what?" Jessica asked, popping out of her reverie and looking at her best friend. Lila was staring at her with crossed arms.

"Your proof!" Lila demanded impatiently.

"Oh, I don't know, it was just . . . nothing. . . ." Jessica said, her words trailing off.

Lila shook her head. "You're really a space case today," she said. "I think you've got water on the brain." She flicked through a rack of bathing suits. "I guess metallic colors are in this season," she said, scrunching up her nose as she sorted through the suits. "Metallic gold, metallic green, metallic blue." She held up a floral-print bathing suit in a metallic orange-pink color. "This color defies description."

Jessica laughed. "Lila, I'm not looking for a bathing suit. I'm looking for a wet suit." She pulled Lila away from the rack. "Now, come on, we don't have all day."

Jessica and Lila made their way to the back of the store, where the selection of surfing attire covered an entire wall. There was a huge assortment of thick, brightly colored rubber wet suits, in all styles and colors. There were biking shorts and tops, knee-length suits with short sleeves, classic full-length suits with long sleeves, solid-colored unitards, cropped pants, and half tops. Jessica took a deep breath, feeling overwhelmed by the selection. Maybe she should have brought Christian with her instead of Lila.

"Hey, Jess, I found your wet suit!" Lila exclaimed.

"Let me see!" Jessica said excitedly.

Lila reached into the rack, pulling out a full-length fluorescent lime-green wet suit. "For you to wear to school after you lose the bet," she said.

"Very funny, Lila," Jessica said, turning back to the rack. "Maybe you should just run up front and purchase some hot-pink oxide for your nose."

"The only place you're going to see me wearing pink oxide is at the beach," Lila retorted.

"We'll see about that," Jessica said lightly. She flicked through the assortment on the rack—red biker shorts with white trim, a brightly colored turquoise-and-white wet suit with solid white sleeves, a classic-style full-length black suit with yellow sleeves . . . Nothing seemed right. She wandered down the aisle, letting her left hand drift through the selection. Then the perfect suit jumped out at her.

"How about this one?" Jessica asked, pulling it out and holding it up for Lila to see. It was a full-length wet suit with short sleeves and a zipper down the front, in electric pink.

"Hot pink?" Lila asked skeptically.

Jessica nodded. "I'm going to try it on." She threw the hanger over her arm and hurried into a free dressing room. Jessica threw off her clothes and wriggled into the tight rubber. It was perfect. The rubber was thick and flexible. She would be warm and insulated in the cold water of the early-morning ocean. Jessica turned and admired herself in the mirror. She looked awesome. Just like a real surfer.

Jessica walked out of the locker room and pirouetted in front of Lila. "What do you think?"

Lila whistled under her breath. "That is totally hot." Then she looked at Jessica, her eyes narrowing suspiciously. "Are you sure you're surfing alone?"

"Of course," Jessica replied lightly.

"Anybody home?" Jessica called as she walked in the front door.

"We're in here!" Elizabeth yelled, glad that Jessica had got home before their meeting adjourned. She was interested in hearing her twin's opinion on their decision to cancel the dance. Elizabeth was hoping she might have got some insider information from Ken. Elizabeth couldn't seem to glean anything from Todd.

Jessica flew into the living room, threw her backpack onto an armchair, and dropped her shopping bags to the floor with a *thud*. Then she rummaged in her cheerleading bag for her pom-poms and threw them onto the floor. Tossing the bag aside, she flopped down onto the rug, using her pom-poms as a pillow.

"Hi, I'm Jessica," she said.

"I guessed," Caitlin replied wryly, and all the girls laughed.

"Jessica, this is Marla and Caitlin from Palisades High," Elizabeth said.

"Uh-oh, the enemy's in the midst," Jessica joked.

"Isn't it crazy?" Marla said. "I've never seen guys get so worked up about a school rivalry."

"Me, either," Jessica said. "I was just talking to Ken about it this afternoon. I think the whole thing's going to come to a head at the dance."

"So do we," Elizabeth said. "We decided to call the dance off."

Jessica shook her head warily. "I don't think I'd do that if I were you."

"We have to," Elizabeth explained. "If we hold the dance, we'll just be providing the setting for a fight."

"I know," Jessica said. "But Ken said the guys

are going to show up at the warehouse no matter what. At least if there's a dance, we might be able to keep things calm."

Elizabeth bit her lip. Jessica was right. Now they had to have the dance. And it was all her fault for coming up with the idea in the first place.

Marla held her head in her hands. "We've created a monster," she groaned.

"There must be something we can do," Elizabeth said, standing up and pacing the room. "I can't bear the thought of just sitting around and watching the guys use our dance as a battleground."

"Maybe the party atmosphere will soothe the guys," Caitlin said optimistically. "Maybe the whole thing will blow over."

Enid shook her head. "I don't think so. The guys at school are getting everybody all worked up."

Elizabeth sighed. "It's true. Soon they'll have the whole student body brainwashed into thinking that Palisades is the enemy."

"The question is, How do we stop them?" Enid wondered.

Suddenly Elizabeth was hit by an idea. She leaned toward her friends, a glint in her eye. "I think we're going to have to fight fire with fire," she said.

"You want to start a rival gang?" Jessica asked in shock.

Elizabeth rolled her eyes. "No, not a rival gang. A rival *force*. We could do positive newspa-

131

per coverage of each other's schools to counter the rivalry."

"Do you really think an article would do the trick?" Marla asked.

"Not an article, an entire edition of the newspaper," Elizabeth replied, her eyes sparkling excitedly. "I think we should both put out special editions of our papers this week with exclusive coverage of the dance and each other's schools. It will raise interest in the dance and create goodwill between the two schools."

The girls nodded enthusiastically.

"For every bad thing the students hear, they'll read a good one," Caitlin said.

"The guys can talk all they want," Marla said. "But we've got the press on our side."

Chapter 9

Early Wednesday morning Jessica dropped her bag onto the sand and faced the turbulent ocean. It was a cold, drizzly day, and the sea was dark and stormy. The entire beach was shrouded in a light gray mist. The waves were huge and angry, crashing against the surf with extraordinary force.

Jessica watched in awe as a raging set of curling waves appeared on the horizon like a water-breathing dragon. Pitching and churning, the massive mountain of water surged and then dashed against the beach in a violent crush of white foam.

A tremor of fear passed through her body as she took in the tumultuous sea. She looked at her watch, wondering if she should wait for Christian. She had got to the beach early. Elizabeth had needed the Jeep for an *Oracle* meeting, so Jessica had borrowed her mother's car. She had told her parents she had an early-morning cheerleading practice.

Jessica shook her head in wonder. A week ago she never would have believed she'd be jumping out of bed every day at five in the morning. But now each day she woke up thinking of riding the waves. It was as if the ocean were calling her. Lila had been right: She did have water on the brain. She loved surfing.

Without giving the stormy day further thought, Jessica plunged into the ocean and waded through the chilly water. She was glad she had on her hot-pink wet suit to keep her warm. She paddled out to sea and caught a wave, enjoying the feel of the cool air rushing at her body. She felt as if she could conquer the world.

A monstrous eight-foot surge came rushing toward her, and she decided to try it. The powerful curling wave gained momentum as it rolled through the ocean, getting bigger and bigger as it reached her. Her chest tightening in anticipation, Jessica positioned herself behind the lip and turned her back to the wave. She pointed the nose of the board down the line and began paddling, springing up as the wave caught her board.

Jessica struggled to maintain her balance as the surging billow carried her high into the air. She was riding beneath the lip of the wave and couldn't seem to get on top of it. Jessica looked down, and fear seized her heart. The ocean was six feet below her. She was riding at the edge of a moving cliff. If she got caught in the thundering current of the surge, she would be crushed.

Tensing the muscles in her legs and holding her arms out, she managed to stay upright on the board. As she soared into the air, she felt the familiar rush of exhilaration course through her body. Raindrops and wind whipped through her hair, and the foamy ocean sprayed her face.

Suddenly the roaring lip of the wave came down on her with all its force, and her surfboard flew out from under her. Jessica went sailing through the air and crashed into the churning water. She struggled to swim but found herself caught in the wild current of the swirling breakers.

Pushing her way up through the heavy water, she desperately tried to surface, only to be knocked down by the next wave. She gasped for breath and swallowed a mouthful of salty green water. Choking and coughing, she somersaulted around crazily, then panicked, kicking her arms and legs out wildly. She felt the world going black around her. *I'm going to drown,* Jessica thought desperately.

As her oxygen thinned, a sense of peace overwhelmed her. She felt light-headed and calm. The surf roared somewhere in the distance. The world became dimmer around her. Jessica closed her eyes and let the water take her, becoming one with the flow of the ocean. Only her senses remained. Cool water, whirling depth . . .

Suddenly she felt a pair of strong arms around

her. Christian was by her side under the water. Kicking through the crosscurrent, he guided her toward the surface. Jessica gasped with relief, gulping in deep mouthfuls of fresh sea air. Her whole body shuddered from the strain, and she violently coughed up salty ocean water.

Treading water, Christian held Jessica in his arms. She relaxed and closed her eyes, enjoying the feel of the cold drizzle falling on her face and the warm security of Christian's arms around her.

Christian wiped her wet hair back from her face. "You OK?" he asked gently.

Jessica nodded, her body still trembling slightly.

Christian looked at her tenderly. "Jessica, you scared me," he said, his voice soft and husky. "I didn't expect to find you out in weather like this. The sea is dangerous in such stormy weather."

Jessica gave him a sheepish smile. "I guess I was a little ambitious, huh?"

Christian nodded. "A little." He shook his head disapprovingly and opened his mouth to say something. Then he shut it quickly, a small smile playing on his lips. Still holding Jessica in his arms, he swam closer to shore.

When they reached shallower water, Jessica slid to her feet. "What were you going to say?" she asked. They waded out of the water and fell onto the sand by the shore. The rain had subsided.

"Nothing," Christian said.

"C'mon," Jessica coaxed. She picked up a stick

and drew a zigzag pattern in the wet sand.

Christian laughed. "I was going to give you a lecture for going out alone in this storm. It's extremely dangerous. Especially for a beginner. But then I realized that I would have done the same thing."

Jessica smiled. "I guess we found each other," she said.

"It's a good thing I found you," Christian said, giving her a reproaching look.

"I thought you said no lecture!" Jessica protested.

"You're right. I won't say another word," Christian said. "But will you just promise me something?"

"What?" Jessica asked.

"Promise me you won't pull a stunt like that again?"

Jessica smiled up at him with twinkling eyes. "Don't worry, I wouldn't do anything you wouldn't do."

Christian groaned. "That's not very reassuring," he said.

Jessica patted his hand. "Don't worry, I think I learned my lesson."

"To tell you the truth, you looked great out there," Christian said. "Just like a real surfer in your new wet suit. That was very impressive. You were riding right under the lip of the wave, and you managed to keep your balance."

"Not for long," Jessica said wryly.

"That's normal," Christian reassured her.

"Every surfer goes down. Wiping out is as much a part of the sport as riding the waves. Surfers spend more time under the water than they do on top of it."

"Well, that's comforting," Jessica said. "I think."

"Actually, it's my fault," Christian said. "I forgot to teach you the most important thing about surfing."

"What's that?" Jessica asked.

"How to wipe out," Christian said.

"There's a technique for crashing?" Jessica asked.

Christian nodded.

"Let's try it," Jessica said.

Christian waggled a wet finger at her. "You have to take a rest first, young lady," he said, admonishing her lightly. "You almost drowned. And besides, I don't want you going out in the rain."

"Why not?" Jessica asked.

Christian grinned. "I don't want you to get wet."

"Elizabeth, if you don't watch it, we're going to have an accident," Olivia said Wednesday morning as Elizabeth raced the Jeep along Valley Crest Road.

Her brakes squealing, Elizabeth skidded wildly around a small blue Toyota and took the ramp onto the highway. Looking quickly into her rearview window, she cut adeptly across four lanes of traffic into the left lane.

Olivia moaned and covered her face with her hands. "Tell me when we get there," she said weakly.

"Oh, sorry," Elizabeth said, lifting her foot off the accelerator and cutting her speed.

She and Olivia were driving to Palisades High to get interviews with the students. Mr. Collins had approved the idea for a special edition of *The Oracle* and had given them a pass to take the morning off. Elizabeth and Olivia were planning to get coverage for an exclusive photojournalism spread of the rival school. Elizabeth was going to write the article, and Olivia was going to shoot pictures.

Elizabeth was wound up with excitement. Ever since she had woken that morning, she had been pumped up with energy. The girls weren't just going to sit back and watch while the guys regressed to the dark ages, taking the whole of Sweet Valley High with them.

"Can I look now?" Olivia asked.

"Of course," Elizabeth said. "We're just coasting gently along the highway."

Olivia peeked through her fingers. "Wow, I can actually see the road now. Before it was just like a blur whizzing before my eyes."

"Oh, Liv, I'm sorry," Elizabeth said. "I guess I was a little overeager."

Olivia sat back hard against the seat. "Whew!" she said, wiping a hand dramatically along her brow. "I think I just lost five years of my life."

Elizabeth laughed.

"What's got into you?" Olivia asked. "You're usually such a careful driver."

"I'm just so excited about doing this spread," Elizabeth said. "It's been so frustrating just sitting around while the guys worked everybody up. At least now we can take action."

"I know. I feel the same way," Olivia said. "I'm psyched that Mr. Collins OK'd the idea. I thought he'd tell us it was impossible to get out an entire edition in two days."

"It's nearly impossible," Elizabeth said. "We're going to have to work like dogs."

"If I know you, nothing's impossible," Olivia said with a grin.

Elizabeth put her foot on the accelerator, gently increasing her speed. She hoped Olivia was right. She didn't want anything to go wrong. Suddenly she glanced over at her friend, her brow creased with worry. "Do we have everything we need?" she asked anxiously.

"Well, let's see, the last time you asked me, we did," Olivia said. "But let me just check again. Maybe something has changed in the last five minutes." She rummaged around on the floor and picked up Elizabeth's supplies. "Here's your notebook. And here is a pencil case full of writing utensils." Then she lifted her camera from around her neck. "Yep, I've still got my camera on me."

Elizabeth smiled abashedly. "So sue me, I'm a perfectionist." Suddenly she saw a sign for Palisades come into view. "Oh, no, that's our exit!" she exclaimed, swerving sharply to the right and cutting through four lanes of traffic at once.

Olivia ducked to the floor. "E-liz-a-beth!"

"Look, Christian, the sun's coming out," Jessica said, pointing to the bright-yellow ball peeking out of the drifting, translucent clouds. The rain had stopped and the sky was a pale blue. The ocean was calm and the waves were almost flat.

"It might end up being a nice day, after all," Christian said, sitting up on the towel.

Jessica sat up with him, feeling refreshed after her nap. She had practically passed out as soon as she'd hit the towel. She hadn't realized how much her accident had drained her. "Let's go wipe out together," she said.

"You got it," Christian said, putting his arms around her and nuzzling her neck. "I'll crash with you any day, baby."

"Christian! I mean in the water," Jessica protested. "Now, c'mon," she said, jumping up and reaching out a hand to him.

Christian gave her a rakish grin. "Oh, the *ocean*," he said as she pulled him to his feet.

As they walked hand in hand to the water's edge, Christian explained the basics of wiping out. "If you get thrown by a big wave, you have to do a duck dive and hug the ocean floor as if your life depended on it."

"A duck dive?" Jessica asked.

"You dive all the way to the ocean floor,"

Christian explained. "Then you hold on to the bottom of the ocean as the water rushes overhead. It's a surfing technique that prevents drowning. You have to wait till the wave subsides before surfacing. If you fight to come up for air, you'll get caught in the crosscurrent and sucked under by the next wave."

They waded into the water and paddled out to sea. Hopping onto their boards, they coasted along a few low waves.

"OK, follow me, Jessica," Christian said. He jumped high in the air and arched his body almost double, cutting into the water straight, like a knife. Jessica quickly dived down after him.

The pressure of the water increased as she swam after Christian. He was floating at the bottom, holding on to the ocean floor. Jessica joined him, digging her hands into the sandy floor of shells and stones and kicking her feet out behind her. It was cold and dark under the sea. And strangely quiet. The water weighed upon her like a great smothering blanket, and the ocean thundered overhead like a distant airplane.

Jessica looked in wonder at the life in the depths of the ocean. The ocean floor was beautiful, a crystal palace of red rocks and seashells. Exotic crustaceans blended in with the sandy bottom. A school of tiny red fish swam in front of her eyes.

For a moment Jessica thought she could stay there forever in this enchanted underworld. A minute later she thought she was going to pass out. Grabbing on to Christian's arm, she pointed upward. Pushing off from the ocean floor, she swam toward the surface with all her might. Her lungs aching, she burst through the foam into daylight.

Jessica grabbed her surfboard and panted for breath. Seconds later Christian surfaced beside her, wrapping a wet arm around her waist.

"It's like paradise down there," Jessica said softly.

"It's like paradise here with you," Christian said, whispering in her ear.

Jessica turned to face him and he wrapped her in his arms, bringing his salty lips toward hers.

"Hi," Elizabeth said with a bright smile, approaching a group of guys in the hall at Palisades High. "We're from Sweet Valley High, and we'd like to do some coverage of your school for our paper."

Elizabeth held out a hand to a lanky guy who was slouched against a locker. "Elizabeth Wakefield," she introduced herself. The guy crossed his arms and looked at her with disdain. Elizabeth dropped her hand to her side, her face burning. The guys around him snickered.

"Why don't you go back where you belong, Elizabeth Wakefield?" the guy said menacingly, looking at her with insolent green eyes.

"Yeah, we don't want any SVH kids in our territory," another guy put in. Long strands of brown hair were falling into his eyes, and contempt was written all over his face.

Elizabeth stared at them openmouthed, stunned at their reaction. She knew the rivalry between the two schools was bad, but she had thought it was contained to members of the football team. Apparently, however, the bad feelings had spread to the entire student body.

But Elizabeth refused to back down. She wasn't going to let a few Palisades guys intimidate her. After all, the whole point of the story was to diminish the rivalry. "The purpose of our article is to show Sweet Valley that Palisades High is more than a football team," Elizabeth explained. "We're trying to create good feelings between the two schools."

The lanky guy laughed, revealing a broken tooth. "Ooh, good feelings."

"Why don't you say we're touchy-feely," his friend suggested sarcastically.

Olivia pulled Elizabeth away. "C'mon, Liz, we're wasting our time with these jerks," she said, giving the guys a steely stare and pivoting on her heel.

The guys laughed as they walked off. "See you at the dance on Friday!" one of them called as they walked away.

Elizabeth was burning with anger. "Can you believe them?" she exclaimed.

"Just ignore them, Liz," Olivia advised. "They're not worth our mental energy. Let's try interviewing some girls. I'm sure they'll be more reasonable."

They turned the corridor and approached a couple of girls hanging out in front of a classroom. From their appearance, Elizabeth guessed they must be freshmen.

"Hi, I'm Elizabeth," Elizabeth said, addressing a small blond girl. "I'd just like to ask you a few questions."

The girl bit her lip and looked at her friend nervously.

"Sorry, we don't have time," her friend said, leading the blond girl away.

Olivia turned to a girl rummaging through a locker. "Hi, my name's Oliv—" she began.

"Sorry, I'm late for class," the girl interrupted, grabbing her books in her arms and running off.

A half hour later Elizabeth felt like a pariah. She and Olivia still hadn't had any luck. They had tried to get interviews with almost every student in the hall, but it was always the same thing. "Sorry, I don't have time." "Sorry, I'm late for class." "Sorry, I don't do interviews."

Elizabeth sighed. "I feel like I'm selling magazines over the phone," she said.

"Nobody will even talk to us," Olivia agreed.

"Olivia, I don't get it," Elizabeth said. "Usually students jump at the chance to get their name in print. But before we even get a sentence out, the kids are running away."

"Well, we're clearly Sweet Valley students," Olivia said.

"But how do they know we're from Sweet Valley? Couldn't we be on the *Pentagon* staff here? Or reporters from another school?" Elizabeth asked, bewildered.

"Liz!" Olivia laughed. "Look at what you're wearing."

Elizabeth looked down at her outfit and laughed as well. "Oh," she said sheepishly. "Good point." She was wearing jeans and a fluffy gray sweatshirt with SWEET VALLEY HIGH written on it in bold block letters.

"OK, time to go under cover," Elizabeth said, handing Olivia her notebook. She pulled the sweatshirt over her head, revealing a yellow T-shirt. Then she turned the sweatshirt inside out.

"There," Olivia said with satisfaction. "Now the idea is to get them talking to us. *Then* we can say we're from Sweet Valley."

"Forget the hall, it's too busy," Elizabeth said. "Let's try some organizations."

Their first stop was the girls' locker room. It was hot and steamy and packed with girls getting ready for gym class. The girls were talking and laughing as they pulled on shorts and T-shirts.

"Let's try the girls on the swim team," Olivia suggested, turning into a damp dressing area. Wet bathing suits were draped over the locker doors, and the girls were wearing racing suits.

"Hi," Elizabeth said, sitting down on the bench next to an athletic-looking girl in a bright-blue bathing cap. "We're putting out a special edition of our paper with exclusive coverage of Palisades High, and we were wondering if we could ask you a few questions."

"Sure!" the girl responded. She smiled a big, friendly smile, eyeing the camera slung around Olivia's neck. "Are you taking pictures?"

"Definitely," Olivia said, unlocking the cap and peering into the lens.

"Hey, I want my picture in the paper, too," a girl with frizzy brown hair said, sitting down with them.

A girl with straight blond hair was standing on the bench, reaching up into a small cubby locker on the top row. "Where are you from?" she asked, turning to look at them.

Elizabeth swallowed nervously. "Uh, we're from Sweet Valley High," she said.

"Oh," the blond girl said, slinging her towel across her shoulders and slamming the locker door shut. She hopped down off the bench and skipped out of the locker room. "See you guys in the pool."

Elizabeth gave Olivia a worried look. "So we'd like to ask you a few questions about the swim team," Elizabeth said, turning to the other two.

The two girls looked at each other nervously.

"Uh, I don't know if that's a good idea," the girl in the bathing cap said, looking around to see if they were being overheard.

"Yeah, sorry." The other girl smiled at her

apologetically. "But, you know, considering the situation . . ." She let the words trail off.

"C'mon," her friend said. "We're going to be late for warm-up."

"See you," the brown-haired girl said. "Good luck!"

Olivia slumped down onto the bench with a sigh.

"Now, c'mon," Elizabeth said encouragingly, taking her hand and pulling her up. "A real journalist never gives up. This is probably good practice for us. It'll give us a taste for what it's like to be in the real world."

Olivia sighed. "I don't think I'm cut out to be a photojournalist. Maybe I should just stick to nature scenes."

"Well, we've got to keep at it," Elizabeth said.

An hour later Elizabeth was ready to give up as well. They had approached practically every organization in the school. They had tried the debating team, the boys' chess club, the girls' glee club, and the track team. They had even tried to talk to some kids in study hall. All their efforts had failed. As soon as they had said they were from Sweet Valley, the kids had backed away as if they had seen a ghost.

"Elizabeth, it's hopeless," Olivia said finally as they wandered back into the main corridor.

Elizabeth sighed. "Maybe we'll have better luck if we don't say we're from Sweet Valley at all."

Suddenly an ominous male voice spoke from behind her back. "So you're the girls from Sweet Valley."

Elizabeth whirled around, and her heart leaped into her throat. Standing in front of her was a gang of tough-looking guys in black leather jackets.

"We've been hearing a lot about you," the guy who had spoken said. He was big and mean looking, with close-cropped hair and a face like a bull's.

"So you'd like to have an interview, would you?" his friend asked. He was a skinny guy with a pale face and stringy red hair. He laughed harshly. "We'll give you an interview, won't we, guys?"

Elizabeth swallowed hard and looked around quickly. The corridor was deserted.

"Your friends at SVH left a nice little message on our football field," the bull-faced guy said menacingly, his beady eyes glinting. "Palisades Pumas Purr Like Kittens." The guy leaned in so close to Elizabeth that she could feel his breath on her face. Elizabeth's eyes widened in fear, and she took a step back. "Well, why don't you tell them we're not purring anymore?"

"Yeah," the skinny guy said. "Tell them we're out for the kill."

Elizabeth nodded and took Olivia by the arm. They walked down the hall as casually as possible, trying not to show their fear. As soon as they turned the corner, they flew down the hall and out the door, running full speed to the Jeep and jumping in.

Elizabeth drove for a few moments in silence, trying to calm the beating of her heart. Then she turned to Olivia, her expression bleak. "It's worse than I thought," she said.

Olivia nodded. "They *want* trouble."

Elizabeth sighed. "Now I know how the guys feel."

"Hey, there's Marla and Caitlin," Olivia said as Elizabeth swung the Jeep into the SVH parking lot.

"They don't look happy," Elizabeth noticed. The girls were sitting on the hood of Marla's white convertible Mustang, waiting for them. Caitlin looked sophisticated, as usual. She had on a black cotton jumpsuit with a scooped-neck white T-shirt underneath and chunky silver jewelry. Marla was dressed casually, wearing a pair of soft faded jeans and a burnt-orange T-shirt. Marla was resting her chin in the palm of her hands, and Caitlin was swinging her feet in a monotonous motion. They couldn't have looked more dejected.

Elizabeth pulled the Jeep into a parking space and the girls hopped out.

"No luck?" Elizabeth asked, walking up to her Palisades friends.

"No luck," Marla confirmed.

"It was unbelievable," Caitlin said, jumping off the hood of the car. "We couldn't get any coverage of SVH students at all."

"Every time we would try to interview somebody, they would start complaining about our school," Marla said. "All they wanted to talk about

150

were the dirty plays at the football game and the egging yesterday."

"And that was just the guys," Caitlin added. "The girls ran away like scared rabbits, as if they were afraid to be seen talking to the enemy."

"It was exactly the same at Palisades," Elizabeth said.

Olivia shook her head. "The guys are angry, and the girls are scared."

"Well, I'm not scared. I'm angry," Elizabeth declared. "I'm not going to let a bunch of high-school boys turn our dance into a war zone."

"Elizabeth is right," Marla stated, her green eyes flashing with determination. "Now it's more important than ever to do positive write-ups of our schools."

"There's just one problem," Olivia pointed out. "Material."

Caitlin sighed. "We don't have any."

"Well, we're just going to have to be creative," Elizabeth said resolutely. "The situation is spiraling out of control. And somebody's got to stop it."

Chapter 10

"Take it all the way in, Jess!" Christian shouted as they rode a huge wave together early Thursday morning.

Skimming the surface of the water, Jessica stayed on top of the swell. She bent her legs and followed the movement of the wave, riding it to the beach. She skidded to a stop as she hit the gravelly sand of the shoreline.

"Race you to the towel!" Jessica cried, jumping off her surfboard and running up the sand. Christian dropped his surfboard and ran after her. Within moments he overtook her. As he was about to reach the towel, Jessica jumped at him and tackled him to the ground. Christian grabbed her in his arms and they rolled around in the sand, kissing passionately.

Laughing, Jessica untangled herself from his

arms and fell on her back onto the towel. She was dripping wet and breathing hard. Christian lay down next to her on his stomach, reaching out a hand to grasp hers.

Jessica closed her eyes, feeling exhausted and exhilarated at the same time. Now surfing really felt natural to her. She could ride a wave with no problem. She was even starting to work on some of the tricks that Christian had taught her.

"I bet I'll be jumping by tomorrow," Jessica boasted, turning a sandy face toward him.

Christian brushed the sand off her cheek. "Well, you're going to have to practice on your own, and then on Saturday you can show me the progress you've made."

"What?" Jessica cried.

"I can't make it tomorrow," Christian explained. I have some stuff to take care of."

"At five in the morning?" Jessica asked.

Christian laughed. "I've been keeping some strange hours. But trust me, by Saturday everything will be fine."

Jessica pouted. A day without Christian seemed like a day wasted. And the surf contest was only three weeks away. Surfing had crept into her blood, but she knew that Christian was part of her new love of the sport, too. Half the fun of mastering moves was showing them to Christian.

But, then, maybe it's for the best, Jessica mused. At least she would be able to semiconcentrate on

Ken if she spent a day apart from Christian. If she didn't see Christian on Friday, maybe he wouldn't be on her mind all weekend. Then she would be able to give Ken more attention on Friday night at the dance. After all, she had resolved to give him all the support he needed.

"Look, the sun is coming up," Christian said, pointing at the horizon. Jessica caught her breath as she looked out across the sea. The pale-blue sky was streaked with bands of red and gold, and the semicircle of the rising sun was a brilliant orange.

Christian sat up and pulled Jessica against him, cradling her body in his arms. Jessica leaned back against his chest, and they watched the sunrise in silence. The bright-orange crescent shone across the sparkling blue water like a highway of brilliant light leading from them to the horizon.

Christian brought his cheek against hers. "I love you, Jessica," he whispered.

Jessica's heart flip-flopped and she felt light-headed. Before she knew what was happening, she heard herself whispering, "I love you, too, Christian."

Christian's arms tightened around her, and Jessica closed her eyes. Even though she knew next to nothing about him, Christian's soul had touched hers. And that was something that happened only once in a lifetime.

"A Palisades Retrospective," Elizabeth wrote at the *Oracle* office on Thursday morning, typing in the title line for her front-page feature article. Then she quickly deleted it. *Could that title be more boring?* she asked herself. *Try again.* "Palisades High: Past and Present." No, that was no good either. Elizabeth sighed. It was the sure sign of a bad article when you started at the beginning. The title was supposed to come last, after the story had been written. But that was the problem. She had no story.

Elizabeth glanced at her watch. She had a half hour before first period. The special edition of *The Oracle* was going to press that afternoon, and Elizabeth and Olivia had to be finished with the article by then. Because they had no new material, the girls had decided to piece together a feature based on Palisades past events.

Using the new on-line computer system, Elizabeth had brought up all the old articles she could find on Palisades High, looking for some trends in Palisades history. Olivia had gathered together old pictures from the photo archives in the *Oracle* office. But so far they hadn't come up with anything.

There must be something we're not seeing, Elizabeth thought, clicking into the on-line computer system. The system allowed her to retrieve stories printed in all the major papers in California over the last fifty years. "Palisades," Elizabeth typed in. Five articles appeared on the screen. She clicked onto the first one with the mouse. It was an article about the Palisades football victory at state a few years ago. She flipped to the next, glancing at the headline. "Palisades Soccer Team Wins at Nationals." She clicked to the third article and skimmed the contents. The basketball team had won the national title. Elizabeth sighed in frustration. Just sports victories. Nothing special.

Elizabeth picked up the tall stack of *Pentagon*s lying on the floor by her side. Marla had dropped off copies of her school paper the previous night, and Elizabeth had spent the whole evening reading through them. She felt as if she knew absolutely everything there was to know about Palisades High. But she was still no closer to writing a positive story about the school.

"Liz, you having any luck?" Olivia asked. She was sitting on the floor in front of a tall green metal file cabinet in the corner of the office. A sea of photographs and negatives surrounded her.

Elizabeth sat back in her chair. "I've almost got the title written," she said with a sigh.

"Uh-oh," Olivia murmured. "Writer's block?"

"No, material block," Elizabeth replied. "I have nothing to say here. Palisades High sounds like every other high school in the country. They have athletic teams, clubs, extracurricular activities . . ." She sat back in her chair. "Liv, we need an angle. What makes Palisades different?"

Olivia rummaged through the photos of Palisades High, picking out the most important shots. "Let's see. A basketball shot, a swimming shot, the debate team, the drama club performing *Macbeth*." Olivia dropped the photos to the floor. "You're right. It could be any school anywhere. Maybe we should title the article 'Palisades: An Entirely Typical High School.'"

Elizabeth threw up her hands in frustration. "Oh, let's just forget it, Olivia. It's futile. We're just going to have to scrap together what we have and put together a general overview of Palisades."

Just then Penny walked into the office. "Letter for you and Olivia," she said, tossing a large manila envelope onto Elizabeth's desk.

"Thanks, Penny." Elizabeth picked up the envelope and looked at it in alarm. Her name and Olivia's were pasted on the front in cut-out blocks of newspaper lettering.

"What is it?" Olivia asked, getting up and pulling over a seat. Elizabeth showed her the front, a grim look on her face.

"Looks ominous," Olivia said quietly. Elizabeth nodded and turned it around. Black ink was scrawled across the seal. "A little gift for the nosy editors of SVH," she read aloud.

Exchanging a nervous glance with Olivia, Elizabeth ripped open the package. A single sheet of construction paper was inside. Elizabeth drew it out with shaking fingers.

The page was a picture of two Roman gladiators engaged in a sword fight. Black paper masks were covering their eyes. The words "SVH

158

Gladiators" were scrawled in red ink across the picture. Above it was a headline written in computer print: "The Deadly Dance: A Duel to the Bloody End."

Elizabeth immediately dropped the picture, as though it had burned her fingers. "What should we do?" she asked.

"I think we should ignore it," Olivia decided. "It's just a stupid prank."

"You're right," Elizabeth agreed, clicking off the computer. She slung her book bag over her shoulder. Elizabeth was in no mood to write her article now. She would have to work on it at lunch. She picked up the sheet of paper and ripped it into little pieces, dropping it into the trash can. "I'll see you at lunch."

"See you later," Olivia said.

Olivia's right, Elizabeth thought as she walked out of the office. *It's just a stupid prank.* But the message the boys from Palisades had written on Ken's street came back to her: "Get ready for your last dance." Elizabeth shivered. Was the letter a prank—or a threat?

Ken threw a bag of chips onto his tray. He was moving through the lunch line mechanically, lost in his own thoughts. All he could think of was the dance the next day. The showdown. He kept picturing a deserted warehouse, and the two groups facing each other in a brutal confrontation. Ken had been wound up all week, waiting for the next move from Palisades. And waiting for the encounter on Friday.

The cafeteria was as crowded and boisterous as usual. The noisy din of lunchroom gossip swirled around him. Chattering students jostled him in the tight line, and impatient hands reached for food all around him. But Ken was oblivious to all of it.

All he saw in front of him was Greg McMullen's face. Greg McMullen's twisted, sneering face as he jeered at him. And all Ken could hear were Greg's taunting words: "Well, if it isn't the little windbag." The words reverberated in Ken's mind. He could feel his blood boiling just thinking about it.

"I said, do you want the lasagna?" a voice barked at him. Ken looked up, startled. It was a dough-faced woman behind the counter, and she appeared to be annoyed.

"Huh? Oh sure," Ken answered. The woman shoved a warm platter across the counter toward him. He grabbed the plate before it teetered over the edge, and dropped it onto his tray.

"Next!" she commanded.

Ken added an apple to his lunch and moved down the line. *Well, it will all be settled at the dance,* he thought. Then the SVH guys would show those Palisades jerks that they weren't wimps. And he and Greg McMullen would have their own private party. Greg was finally going to get what was coming to him. Ken couldn't wait.

Ken grabbed some silverware from the utensil bin and headed to a table, imagining the satisfaction of giving McMullen a taste of his own medicine. He could feel the adrenaline rushing through his veins as he methodically pounded the guy in the stomach.

Suddenly Bruce and Aaron converged on him from either side. They were carrying trays with sandwiches from the à la carte line. Their faces were grim.

Ken was immediately on guard. He could sense that something had happened. "What's up?" Ken asked.

"Palisades has struck again," Bruce said.

Ken's eyes narrowed. "What have they done now?"

"They took another one of our guys out at the tennis tournament last night," Aaron said.

Ken swore under his breath. "The Palisades teams should be banned from playing sports," he said. "What happened?"

"Wayne Williamson, the tennis player on the Palisades team, beamed the ball at Tom McKay during their match." Bruce's green eyes glittered angrily. "He aimed right for his head. McKay went down on the turf, and they called the match."

Ken shook his head. "Unbelievable," he said.

"It is unbelievable," Aaron agreed. "Nobody gets hit on the head in tennis."

"Not unless it's deliberate," Bruce added.

"Is McKay hurt?" Ken asked.

"He'll be all right," Bruce admitted. "He suffered some light injuries and a concussion." Bruce grabbed a handful of silverware and threw it onto his tray with a loud clatter. "He was lucky," he growled. "Luckier than Williamson's going to be."

"OK, let's see what we've got for our exclusive edition," Penny said during lunch period. The *Oracle* staff was having a special meeting to put together the special edition of the newspaper. Penny was propped up on a stool in front of the drafting desk, the material spread out in front of her. Mr. Collins was sitting at a table with John Pfeifer, the sports editor. Olivia was on the floor, pasting up the spread for the Palisades retrospective.

"Penny, I'll be with you in just a sec," Elizabeth called. She was sitting behind her computer, furiously typing in the final paragraph of the Palisades feature.

"OK, Liz," Penny said, turning her attention to the group. She fished through the papers on the desk. "We've got Elizabeth's 'Personal Profiles' column on Marla Davidson, the editor in chief of the Palisades *Pentagon,* John's coverage of the football game last week against the Palisades Pumas, Elizabeth's piece on the upcoming dance . . ."

Elizabeth was half listening as she typed in the final words of the article. She had never written a feature article so fast. She and Olivia had raced to the *Oracle* office when the bell had rung after

French class. They had been working intensely for the past hour.

"And Elizabeth and Olivia's retrospective." Penny stopped and looked over at Elizabeth. "Liz, do you think you're going to make this edition?"

"One minute!" Elizabeth said, holding up an index finger. She typed in the final words with lightning-quick fingers. She ran a spell check on the article and quickly skimmed the contents on the screen, looking for typos. Then she printed it out. She pulled it out of the printer and jumped up.

"Voilà," she said, flourishing the piece. Olivia stood, too, simultaneously holding up her completed layout.

"Wow, what a team," said Penny, shaking her head admirably. "That's what I call working under pressure."

"You guys are really going to go places," John said.

Penny rubbed her hands together. "Great. Looks like we're all set," she said. "The paper's going to press this afternoon. I'm going to need some help today after school. Can any of you make it?"

Suddenly the door flew open and Bruce and Ken stormed into the office.

"We heard you're running a special edition of *The Oracle* about Palisades," Bruce said.

"That's right," Penny said. "Can we help you?"

"We've got some material to be covered in the special edition," Ken said. "Some late-breaking news."

Elizabeth listened worriedly as Bruce recounted what had happened at the tennis tournament. It was one more event to incite the wrath of the SVH guys. And if the news of the latest incident got out, the students would be out of control by the time of the dance.

"That Williamson jerk took Tom McKay out on purpose," Bruce said, his eyes flashing angrily. "And I want the whole school to know about it."

"Unfortunately, it's too late," Elizabeth said, jumping in quickly. "The paper's going to press today. We've already got all the material together."

"No, it's OK," John said. "I could probably write up a quick column during my study period." Elizabeth's heart sank. The last thing they needed was negative coverage. It was bad enough that the news would travel by ear. "You think you could give me a quick interview this afternoon, Bruce?"

"You got it," Bruce said, smiling with satisfaction.

"See you," Ken said, and he and Bruce left the office.

After the door had swung shut behind Ken and Bruce, Elizabeth turned nervously to John. "John, I don't think you should cover the tennis match in the special edition."

John turned to her in surprise. "Why not?"

"It will only incite the rivalry further," Elizabeth explained.

"Elizabeth, that's irrelevant," John insisted. "The tennis match is news and we have to cover it.

It's our job to be objective and report the facts."

"But an injury during a tennis match isn't newsworthy," Elizabeth protested. "That kind of thing happens all the time. The only reason we would be covering it is because it concerns the rivalry."

John stood up, fire in his eyes. "Exactly," he said. "The rivalry is news, and it's the only thing worth covering." He paced the floor in agitation. "In fact, we should have included a feature article on the rivalry between the schools, and the sports pieces should focus on the supposed dirty play by the Palisades players."

"But the rivalry has nothing to do with Palisades as a whole. It's only a conflict between a small group of troublemakers," Elizabeth argued. "If we cover the rivalry, then we'll be presenting a slanted picture of the school. That would be slander."

"Elizabeth, the rivalry is news and you know it. It's irrelevant if it concerns a small group." John picked up the Palisades retrospective and skimmed through it. "Palisades High, a well-rounded school . . . success in sports . . . a winning newspaper staff . . ." John scoffed, and threw it aside. "This shouldn't even be printed. It isn't newsworthy at all."

Elizabeth bit her lip. She knew he was right. The rivalry was news. The rest was just filler. But if they covered the rivalry, they would only enhance the antagonism between the schools. Elizabeth was torn. For once she felt that her journalistic standards were coming into conflict with her ethics.

"Whoa, whoa," Penny said, holding up a hand. "Why don't we let Mr. Collins mediate?"

Elizabeth turned to Mr. Collins hopefully. "Mr. Collins, what do you think?"

"Elizabeth, I think you know what I'm going to say," he said, looking at her apologetically.

Elizabeth sighed. "Objectivity is the number-one principle in journalism," she recited. "We don't make the news, we just report it."

Mr. Collins nodded and John beamed. Elizabeth's lip was trembling. She had helped make this news, and now she had to report on it. She felt as if she were caught in a vicious circle from which she couldn't escape. No matter what her intentions, she only seemed to provoke the antagonism between the two schools. All her efforts kept backfiring.

"That doesn't mean the rivalry is all we cover," Mr. Collins said. "It's just part of the picture, and it'll be an editorial. Elizabeth and Olivia's retrospective will get front page."

Chapter 11

"It's worse than I feared," Elizabeth said to Olivia as they walked out of the cafeteria on Friday. "Our special edition on Palisades is just getting everybody all worked up about the rivalry."

The Oracle had come out that morning, and Sweet Valley High was in a frenzy—the edition had only served to fuel the fire. Ever since John's articles had hit the news bins, everybody seemed to be outraged. Everywhere she looked, somebody's nose was stuck in the paper. All anybody was talking about was the cheap plays by Palisades at the football and tennis games.

Olivia shook her head. "It's a nightmare," she said. "The whole thing completely backfired. Instead of creating good feelings between the schools, it just made the situation worse."

Elizabeth swung through the cafeteria doors,

frustrated that their attempt had failed. Then she stopped in shock. Everywhere she looked, the halls were plastered with photocopies of *The Oracle*'s sports articles and of John's editorials on the football game and the tennis match. The boys had obviously been busy during lunch.

"I can't believe this," Elizabeth said, ripping the articles off the wall and storming down the hall.

They turned the corner to their lockers, and Elizabeth's mouth dropped open. An entire wall of lockers was covered with the headlines of the sports articles, which had been copied and enlarged: "Palisades Pumas Play Dirty" and "Final Score: Hate Hate."

"Would you look at this?" Elizabeth cried, waving a hand in the air. "It's like a propaganda film."

"Wow, they're really trying to indoctrinate everybody," Olivia agreed. She pointed to the covered lockers. John's tennis article was pasted up in even rows. "Hate Hate" seemed to scream out from the wall.

"I knew this would happen," Elizabeth swore. "I knew we shouldn't let John do sports coverage."

Elizabeth swiped at the locker, ripping off a whole row of articles at once. She crumpled up the paper and threw it into a recycling bin. Olivia helped her until they had torn down all of the headlines.

"It's as if we didn't even write our articles," Elizabeth said despondently. "All anyone can see is this."

"No, they can see ours, too," Olivia said angrily, pointing to the opposite wall.

Elizabeth followed her gaze. Their retrospective was also adorning the walls, but a big *X* had been drawn over the article. The headline had been rewritten with red marker: "Wipe out Palisades History."

Elizabeth ripped the pages off the wall, her anger growing. "I have never seen such an abuse of journalism in my life," she raged. "Look, there's another one!" she cried as her eyes lit on another copy of their retrospective.

She was reaching up to rip an article off the wall when she felt a hand lock itself around her wrist. Elizabeth turned angrily, shaking off the hand. It was Bruce and he was scowling. Aaron and Ronnie were standing by his side. They were all wearing their jean jackets and dark glasses.

"Hey, what do you think you're doing?" Bruce snarled.

"You're destroying our artwork," Aaron protested.

Elizabeth was outraged. "Your artwork! This is *our* work!"

"These are important documents," Ronnie said. "We had to do a lot of work to decorate the halls like this."

"You think these are just decorations?" Elizabeth asked angrily. "You're supposed to *read* the articles, not make a collage out of them."

"We read them, all right," said Bruce. "And now we want to make sure everybody else reads them, too. Or at least *some* of the articles."

"How dare you?" Elizabeth asked, turning to

face him. Her eyes were flashing. "You're using *The Oracle* to brainwash everybody in the school."

"Hey, it's public property," Bruce replied. "We can do whatever we want with it."

"That's right," Elizabeth said angrily, ripping down the article. "And so can I."

"You a Palisades fan or something?" Bruce jeered.

Elizabeth sighed. Obviously anger wasn't getting her anywhere. They didn't seem to get the point. She tried to appeal to reason. "Bruce, don't you see what you're doing? You're turning this dance into a war zone."

"You guys are creating a really dangerous situation," Olivia added. "Somebody's going to end up getting hurt."

Bruce looked at the other guys and snickered. "You know, I think the girls are right. Why don't we call the Palisades guys tonight and make up? Then we can all get together and have a tea party."

"Ooh," Aaron squealed, clapping his hands together. "That sounds like such fun."

Elizabeth threw up her hands. "It's hopeless, Olivia," she said. "Let's go."

"The boys are beyond the point of sanity," Olivia remarked as they walked off.

Elizabeth shook her head. "Their hormones have gone into overdrive."

Elizabeth stormed into the *Oracle* office Friday after school and slammed the newspaper on the table. "Mr. Collins, have you seen what's going on out there?" she asked. "Our special edition is covering the walls."

Mr. Collins nodded. "I noticed," he replied wryly.

"Can they do that?" Elizabeth asked. "Do they have a right to do that?"

He nodded again. "Of course. It's the downside to freedom of speech."

"But this isn't freedom of speech," Elizabeth protested. "It's brainwashing. They're using *The Oracle* for propaganda purposes."

"Liz, there's nothing we can do about that," Mr. Collins said. "Our job is just to report the facts."

"But they're *twisting* them," Elizabeth wailed.

"Remember, Liz, the public is not as gullible as you think," Mr. Collins said reassuringly. "They can read between the lines." He picked up the front page ruefully. "Or behind the *X*'s."

But Elizabeth shook her head. "I don't know, Mr. Collins," she said. "In this case, I don't think so."

Mr. Collins looked at her thoughtfully. "What do you mean, Liz?"

"I think we're dealing with mass mentality here—a *mob*," Elizabeth said, biting her lip worriedly. "We're dealing with a group gone completely out of control."

"Enid, can you read that sign?" Elizabeth asked as they tried to find a turnoff street on their way to the warehouse to decorate for the dance. Even

171

though it was only six o'clock, it was already dark outside, and a light drizzle was falling. The road was shrouded in a gloomy fog.

Enid peered into the mist. "Something Avenue," she read.

"I hope that wasn't our turn," Elizabeth said. They'd been driving for the past half hour, and they kept getting lost. Elizabeth wasn't familiar with this part of town, and it was difficult to read the road signs in the rain.

"At this rate, we'll never get there," Enid said, shifting impatiently in her seat.

"Maybe that's just as well," Elizabeth replied. It seemed as though they were driving into an abyss. Elizabeth felt as if she had set the wheels of some horrible machine in motion, and now there was no way to stop it.

"It should be right around here," Elizabeth said. "Enid, can you look at the map?" Marla had drawn a map for them with directions to the warehouse.

After flicking on the overhead light, Enid picked up the map and studied it. "This should be it," she said as they reached the next intersection.

Elizabeth slowed to a stop and peered through the dense fog. The sign was covered with branches. She pulled the Jeep to a halt and jumped out. Wet leaves crunched underneath her feet. Elizabeth pulled back the branches and looked at the sign. Phantom Lane. Her mouth went dry as she read it. She broke off the branches so the rest of the kids could find the warehouse. *Although we'd all be better off if I didn't bother,* she thought.

"That's it," Elizabeth said, climbing back into the Jeep and revving the engine. She maneuvered the car carefully down the winding lane.

As Elizabeth pulled the Jeep into the gravel parking lot, a sense of foreboding overcame her. The warehouse was in a deserted corner of a run-down industrial area. It seemed fitting that it was located midway between the two towns, Elizabeth thought. *In the middle of nowhere.* She shivered. She felt as though they had entered the Twilight Zone.

Elizabeth climbed out of the Jeep, then reached into the back for a big canvas bag. "Enid, I've got our dresses," she said. They were both wearing jeans to decorate in, and they had brought their formal clothes with them. Elizabeth and Enid had been so caught up with party preparations that they hadn't bothered making costumes. Caitlin and Marla had said they would make masks for all of them.

"Great," Enid told Elizabeth. "I'll bring the food." Enid opened the passenger door and picked up a couple of grocery bags from the floor. Her arms full, she slipped out of the Jeep and kicked the door shut with her foot.

The two girls crossed the gravel lot and pushed open the heavy steel door, entering the vast wooden space.

What were we thinking? Elizabeth wondered as

she took in the spooky surroundings. The warehouse was a damp, dusty space with wooden floors and no windows. It was illuminated by one lightbulb hanging from a cord in the ceiling and long white candles on a rectangular table. The wooden cavern reminded Elizabeth of the big gaping mouth of a jack-o'-lantern. *This is no place for a dance,* Elizabeth thought. *It looks like a haunted house.*

Marla and Caitlin were already there, hanging up decorated masks on the wooden beams of the walls. They were both dressed in Catwoman disguises, black unitards with tails, and had whiskers painted on their faces.

"You made it," Marla said, turning to give them a smile. She climbed down from her perch on a rickety ladder, careful not to trip on her tail.

"It wasn't easy," Enid said. She set the grocery bags down on the table.

"Hi, you guys," Caitlin said in a lackluster voice, leaning against a wooden beam. Both of the Palisades girls had grim expressions on their faces.

"Sorry we're late," Elizabeth said. "We had some trouble getting here."

"Maybe the guys will have trouble getting here, too," Marla said hopefully.

"You two look great," Elizabeth said, trying to sound enthusiastic.

"Thanks," Marla said with a smile. "And you look—"

"Casual," Caitlin put in.

174

Elizabeth held up their bag of clothes. "We're going to change later."

"We should have thought of that," Marla said. "I keep snagging my costume on the splintery wood in this place."

Caitlin walked over to the table and picked up a black mask. She pulled it over her head and adjusted the band. The eyeholes slanted upward, creating an effect of mystery. "What do you think?"

"Nice," Elizabeth enthused. "You look just like a cat."

Caitlin laughed. "Good, because that's what I'm supposed to be." She handed a pair of masks to Enid and Elizabeth. "Here are yours."

"Thanks a lot for making them," Elizabeth said. She put her mask over her head and let it fall around her neck.

Marla stood back with her hands on her hips. "I thought the warehouse would be the perfect setting for the dance, but we can't seem to achieve a party atmosphere," she said. "The masks on the wall just look spooky."

"Yeah," Elizabeth agreed. "I feel like we should have a seance here and try to communicate with ancient spirits."

"That would probably be more fitting," Caitlin said wryly.

"Well, we're just going to have to transform the place," Marla decided with determination.

"Why don't Enid and I take over the decorations?" Elizabeth suggested.

"OK, we'll set up the refreshments," Caitlin said.

Half an hour later the girls had finished. Elizabeth stepped back to survey their work. She and Enid had covered the walls and the table with colorful paper streamers. Big helium balloons floated from the ceiling beams. Marla and Caitlin had set out plates of bread, cheese, fruit, and chips on the refreshment table. An elegant white tablecloth draped the table, and a big glass bowl of fruit punch sat in the middle.

Elizabeth couldn't understand it. They had set up classic party decorations, but they couldn't seem to create a festive environment. The hanging lightbulb cast eerie shadows on the streamers on the wall, and the food twinkled eerily in the light from the flickering white candles. The helium balloons looked like dancing ghosts with dangling legs. A shroud of gloom hung over the place.

"So what do you think?" Marla asked.

The girls looked at each other in despair. "It'd be perfect for Halloween," Caitlin said. "Too bad that's months away."

Elizabeth shrugged. "Oh, well," she said. "There's nothing we can do about it. Maybe the atmosphere will liven up when people get here."

Elizabeth grabbed the last decoration—a banner to hang over the door—and went outside. As she reached up to secure the sign, the wind whipped through her hair and sent the sign rippling awkwardly. It was beginning to rain.

Standing on her toes, Elizabeth fastened the banner firmly to the molding with thumbtacks.

She stepped back to look at it, reading the Gothic-style red letters: WELCOME TO THE SVH-PH MASKED BALL! But then the words began to blur in the rain, and Elizabeth remembered another sign, one that now caused her to tremble involuntarily. *The Deadly Dance: A Duel to the Bloody End.*

Chapter 12

"I think that's it," Jessica said to Ken, pointing to a crooked road sign ahead. Ken slowed the car and coasted up to the sign. Jessica unrolled the window and leaned out into the wet, windy night. A gust of wind whipped her hair across her face. Flicking her hair out of her eyes, she squinted to read the sign. "Phantom Lane," she affirmed.

Ken nodded and steered the car silently to the right. *How appropriate,* Jessica thought, wiping her wet face with the back of her arm. *Phantom Lane.* The whole atmosphere of the road was weird and eerie.

Ken switched on the headlights, maneuvering the car carefully down the twisting road. Suddenly a bolt of lightning illuminated the sky, and the clouds burst forth in a clap of thunder. Rain fell in a steady patter, blanketing the car. Ken switched on the windshield wipers and peered through the curtain of rain, intent on his driving.

Jessica looked over at Ken nervously. His eyes were narrowed to slits, and his fingers gripped the steering wheel so tightly that his knuckles were white. Jessica could practically feel the tension emanating from his body. Ken was wound up like a coil, and he looked as if he were ready to spring.

Jessica didn't know when she had seen Ken so distracted. He was completely preoccupied, lost in his own world. He had barely spoken the whole way there. She had tried to make conversation, but he had answered her only in monosyllables. Finally she had given up. They had driven through the drizzle in silence, each lost in thought.

Jessica sighed. She had resolved to back Ken in his time of need, but he didn't seem to want her support. She couldn't reach him. It was as if he had become a stranger.

And so have I, Jessica thought. No matter how she tried not to think about Christian, he kept popping into her mind. He hadn't been on the beach that morning, and she had gone surfing alone. She missed him already. She ached to be with him in the ocean.

Jessica closed her eyes for a moment. The weekend stretched out endlessly before her. She wished the evening were over. She was in no mood for a school dance. She would rather be in bed, listening to the rain and dreaming of Christian. She wanted to keep her eyes closed, drift off to sleep, and wake up on Monday morning.

Suddenly Ken pulled the car to a quick halt, abruptly breaking Jessica's reverie. They were in a big parking lot at a huge warehouse. A banner was hanging over the vast steel door: WELCOME TO THE SVH-PH MASKED BALL! It was waving in the wind, its red letters blurred by the rain. It looked as if the sign were crying bloody tears.

"Let's go," Ken said, grabbing his mask from the seat and jumping out of the car. He pulled on his black denim jacket and yanked a black ski mask down over his head. He was wearing black jeans and a white T-shirt, and his face was almost entirely hidden by the black mask. Jessica shivered as she took in his attire. Ken looked like some kind of gangster. *He isn't dressed for a dance*, she realized. *He's dressed for battle*.

Jessica stepped out of the car, picking up her bag and adjusting her clothes. She was wearing a short black rayon halter dress that tapered at the waist and flared into a skirt. She had made a mask, but she hadn't bothered with a costume. Usually Jessica went all out for masquerade parties, but this time she couldn't summon up the enthusiasm. She slammed the door shut and hurried after Ken. He was standing at the door, tapping a foot impatiently.

Ken opened the door for her as she reached it. "Thanks," Jessica said, ducking under his arm. She unzipped her shoulder bag and pulled out her

181

mask. It was glittery turquoise with sequins. A black stick was attached to the side.

"So what do you think?" Jessica asked, turning to Ken and holding the mask up to her face.

"Huh? Nice," Ken replied.

Jessica shook her head. Ken really was in another world tonight. Usually she would have been offended by his lack of attention. After all, she was wearing a new dress and she had made an exotic mask. But tonight she didn't really care. She just wanted to get through the evening.

"Wow, it's packed here," Jessica said as she and Ken walked into the warehouse.

The Droids were up on a wooden platform, playing one of their most popular numbers, and the dance floor was already crowded with masked dancers. The band members were in costume as the Flintstones. They were all dressed like cavemen, with leopard-print outfits and matching masks. Dana Larson, the lead singer, held a big bone in her hand, and she had another bone entwined in her hair.

Ken headed straight for the floor, but Jessica pulled him back. "Ken, we've got to get in line first," she reminded him. "You've got the tickets, right?"

Ken nodded, and they walked to the back of the line, which wound all the way across the floor. Jessica couldn't believe how crowded the event was. Even with admittance at ten dollars a head, it seemed as if everyone from both high schools had turned out.

"Everybody's really gone all out with the masks," Jessica noticed as they took their places in line. She saw a number of Batmans, a werewolf, and a Dracula. There were several exotic masks as well—Greek-tragedy masks, Japanese-drama masks, and carnival masks. Others had come in full costume. Winston and Maria were dressed as Louis XVI and Marie Antoinette, and it looked as if all the members of the royal family had turned out for the occasion. Jessica noticed a number of Queen Elizabeths and a couple dressed as Prince Charles and Princess Diana.

"Mm," Ken grunted.

Jessica rolled her eyes. Trying to talk to him was useless. The line moved quickly, and soon they were at the door. Enid was frantically collecting the tickets. She was wearing a midnight-blue velvet dress and a black cat mask.

"Hi, Enid," Jessica said. "Are you Catwoman?"

"All the members of the dance committee are," Enid said. "Where's your mask?"

Jessica held her mask up to her face. "Wow, that's really beautiful," Enid said. "Did you make it yourself?"

"Of course," Jessica said with a smile.

"Did you buy tickets in advance, or do you want to buy them now?" Enid asked, picking up a notebook and scanning her list. "Oh, here you are."

"Ken's got the tickets," Jessica said, looking over at him. He was peering into the crowd with narrowed eyes.

"Ken!" Jessica said, nudging him. "The tickets."

"Oh, right," Ken mumbled, fishing in his pocket and handing the tickets to Enid, his eyes on the crowd the whole time.

Jessica shivered as they entered the space, wrapping her arms around her body. "It's spooky in this place," she said. The vast warehouse was bathed in a dim white light, and dust particles hovered in the air. The air was damp, and the steady patter of rain could be heard.

The rain reminded her of the morning she had surfed in the storm alone. The morning that Christian had saved her. She could feel his strong arms around her as he guided her to the surface. And she could feel his wet, salty lips on hers as he kissed her. Her body tingled at the thought of it.

Then she shook her head hard, forcing her thoughts away from Christian. She was there at the dance with Ken, not on the beach with Christian. She repeated her resolve to give Ken all her support in his time of need. She had to give him all her attention tonight.

Jessica touched his arm softly. "Ken, are you all right?"

Ken nodded, his eyes intent on the crowd.

Suddenly a pang of nervousness hit Jessica. "Ken, could we talk for a minute?"

"What is it?" he asked, looking impatient.

She led him to a corner of the room. "Ken, would you promise me something?" Jessica pleaded.

"What?" he asked.

Jessica touched the edge of his arm. "Could you promise me not to fight tonight?"

Ken turned to look at her, a serious expression in his eyes. "Jessica, I'm sorry, that's one promise I can't make."

Jessica bit her lip. She didn't know what had got into Ken. He was acting totally out of character. Ken was usually so peaceful. But now he was acting just like the rest of the guys. He seemed to be blindly driven by a thirst for revenge.

"Could you at least try not to initiate anything?" Jessica begged.

Ken shook his head. "Jessica, I've got a debt to pay. And I'm going to pay it," he said grimly. "Usually I think it's best to turn the other cheek, but there are limits to what a man can take. I think I've reached my limit."

Jessica sighed. It was obviously impossible to talk him out of it. Then she made a new resolve. She would stay by his side all night. She would stick to him like glue. And she would tell Elizabeth and Maria to do the same with Todd and Winston. After all, if the girls were there, the guys wouldn't fight. The key was not to let the guys be alone.

"C'mon, Jessica, let's go," Ken said, pulling her toward the crowd. They had just reached the dance floor when Bruce appeared in front of them.

"Hey, Matthews," Bruce said. Ken nodded.

"Hi, Bruce," Jessica said, raising her mask to her face and peering at him through the eyeholes.

Bruce looked at Jessica and snorted. "What are you, a bruise?"

Jessica lowered her mask, looking at him in disdain. "What are you talking about?"

"Your costume," Bruce said, chortling. "It's black and blue."

"Bruce, sometimes you are so stupid, it defies comprehension," Jessica shot back, rolling her eyes and looking away.

Jessica scanned the room for Lila and Amy, but the warehouse was so dark and crowded that she could barely recognize anyone. Then she looked back at the entrance, hoping to catch sight of Elizabeth. She wanted to warn her to stay by Todd's side. But Enid was sitting by the table at the door alone.

Well, she would find her friends later. It was probably best to dance now. It would help Ken to relax and would help get her mind off Christian. And it would keep Ken out of trouble as well.

"Ken, let's dance," she said, turning to him. Then she looked around wildly. "Ken?"

But Ken was gone. He and Bruce had disappeared into the sea of masked dancers.

"Are we all here?" Bruce asked.

Ken looked around at the group quickly. He

was standing in a dark corner with Bruce, Aaron, Ronnie, Todd, and Winston. They were all dressed in black jeans, and they were all wearing black ski masks. "Yeah, we're all here," Ken said.

Ken's whole body was tensed. Ever since he had walked into the dance, he had been on guard, waiting for something to happen. He hadn't seen any of the Palisades guys yet, but he knew they were there. He could feel it in his blood. And he was ready for them. The latest incident with the tennis match had sent Ken over the edge. He was itching for a fight.

"Great," Bruce said, his eyes gleaming. "Time for a little action." He rubbed his hands together. "Let's go find our pals from Palisades. I've got a little thank-you present to give them."

Winston shuffled from one foot to the other, a nervous expression on his face. "I don't know if this is such a good idea," he said. "Somebody could really get hurt."

Bruce looked at him and sneered. "That's the whole point, Egbert. Pain for Palisades—remember?"

"Maybe we should just try to talk to them," Winston suggested.

Bruce laughed a harsh, bitter laugh. "I'll talk to them, all right," he replied. "With my *fists*."

Todd didn't look too pleased about the prospect of starting a fight either. "Look, Bruce, calm down a little. The dance just started. Let's just wait and see what happens."

Without warning a group of Palisades guys appeared. They were big, hulking guys, and they looked like a bunch of punks. They were wearing black jeans and black leather jackets. They all had on black masks as well.

"Well, if it isn't our little friends from Sweet Valley," Greg McMullen said, his voice dripping with sarcasm.

Ken bristled at the sound of his voice. He could feel the blood coursing through his veins. He fought the urge to send his fist flying into McMullen's jaw.

"What are you doing hiding in the corner?" Greg jeered. "Afraid we would find you?"

Bruce crossed his arms over his chest, and his eyes narrowed to little slits. "We were just waiting for you," he said, his voice calm and threatening.

"You have something you want to tell us?" a hulking guy said, stepping up to Bruce and sneering in his face.

Bruce didn't back down. "As a matter of fact, we do," he replied, staring the guy down. "But I don't think we can put it in words." He clenched a fist ominously.

"Is that a threat?" Greg McMullen asked.

Ken stepped up to Greg. When he spoke, his words were slow and deliberate. "That's not a threat, McMullen. That's a promise."

Greg cackled loudly, laughing right in Ken's face. "So the little windbag can speak."

Greg's laughter sent Ken into a blind fury. He

saw red and jumped at Greg wildly, swinging a fist at his face. Greg leaped adeptly out of the way, and Bruce pulled Ken back.

Ken struggled, broke free from Bruce, and faced Greg squarely, his fists clenched into tight balls at his sides. "What's wrong?" he challenged him. "You can only dish it out? You afraid to fight?"

"I don't think this is the place," Greg returned. "I wouldn't want to dirty the dance floor with your blood."

Bruce stepped between them before Ken could respond. "Why don't we take this outside?" he suggested.

Elizabeth pushed her way through the crowded warehouse, desperately searching for Todd. He had given her a quick kiss when he'd arrived, and then he had disappeared into the corner with the rest of the guys. But now they were nowhere to be seen. Elizabeth had a gut feeling that something was terribly wrong.

Suddenly she felt a hand at her elbow. She turned and saw a cute guy with curly brown hair. He was dressed like Sherlock Holmes, with a plaid cap on his head and a pipe in his mouth. "Cheerio, Catwoman! Might I have this dance?" he asked in a British accent.

"Sorry, don't have time," Elizabeth said, pushing her mask around her neck and hurrying away. She weaved through the crowd and made her way to the far end of the room, walking as quickly as she could in

189

her skirt and heels. She was wearing a long, straight black skirt and a mint-colored silk blouse. She wished she had worn another outfit. The skirt kept tangling itself between her legs, and she was forced to take small steps. She stopped and hopped out of her heels, grabbing her shoes in her right hand.

She reached the far corner of the room and waited a moment, letting her eyes adjust to the dim light. It was dark and dusty at the periphery of the room. Feeling her way along the wall, Elizabeth did an entire circuit of the warehouse, moving from corner to corner. All she found was cobwebs and spiders.

Elizabeth coughed and waved the dust out of her eyes. The only place left was the dance floor. *Maybe they're hidden in the middle of the floor,* Elizabeth hoped. Hurrying across the cold floor, she joined the crowd and made her way to the throng of dancers. Snatches of conversation reached her ears, and she could hear the light tinkling of laughter. It looked as if everybody was having a good time.

Elizabeth peered into the crowd, hoping to catch sight of any of the guys. She wanted to kick herself for having even come up with the idea of a masquerade party—she couldn't recognize anyone. And the disguises only added to the eerie atmosphere. It was like some horrible ghostly ball.

"Olivia?" Elizabeth asked, tapping the shoulder of a dancing girl with frizzy brown hair. The girl pulled off her mask and looked at her. It wasn't Olivia.

"Oh, sorry," Elizabeth apologized.

Then she caught sight of Annie Whitman and Cheryl Thomas. They were dressed as Amazon queens, wearing long togas that went over one shoulder and carrying bows and arrows. She pushed her way through the crowd toward them.

"Hi, Liz!" Annie waved.

"Great party!" Cheryl shouted over the music. "Unbelievable turnout."

"Thanks," Elizabeth said. "Listen, have you guys seen Todd?"

They shook their heads. "Actually, I haven't seen any of the guys all night," Annie replied. "Do you think they showed up?"

Elizabeth nodded her head. "I wish they hadn't," she said, her face grim. "Listen, if you see Todd, can you tell him I'm looking for him?"

"Sure," Annie promised.

"And would you tell him it's . . . important?"

Annie looked at her with concern. "Liz, is everything all right?"

Elizabeth nodded. "For the moment," she answered.

Elizabeth rushed off and barreled into Olivia. She was slow-dancing with her boyfriend, Harry Minton, an art student at a nearby college. They were disguised as Cleopatra and Mark Antony. Olivia was wearing a stunning long emerald-green dress, and she looked like an Egyptian queen. A straight black wig with bangs covered her wild hair, and thick black eyeliner accentuated her hazel eyes. Harry had on a Roman-style toga and a simple black mask.

"Whoa!" Olivia said, laughing.

"Hey, Liz, do you want to join us?" Harry teased.

"Oh, sorry," Elizabeth said. "Have you guys seen Todd around?"

Harry shook his head, and Olivia, looking concerned, asked, "Is something wrong?"

Elizabeth's expression was grim. "I don't know," she said. "I can't find the guys anywhere." A feeling of panic mounted in her.

Olivia touched her arm. "Listen, I'll keep an eye out on the dance floor," she said.

"Thanks, Liv," Elizabeth said. "I'll see you later."

Elizabeth elbowed her way through the dancers, feeling at a loss. She didn't know where to look next. The boys were clearly not on the dance floor. But, then, she hadn't really expected to find them there. That left only one possibility. They were outside. A sick feeling settled in the pit of Elizabeth's stomach.

Elizabeth left the dance floor and headed to the door. Enid was still sitting at the table, accepting tickets from late arrivers.

"Enid, have you seen Todd?" Elizabeth asked.

Enid shook her head. "Not since he came in."

"What about the other guys?" Elizabeth asked.

Enid looked worried. "They all got here early, and I haven't seen them since."

Elizabeth was bewildered. They weren't anywhere

to be found in the warehouse, and they hadn't left, either. Where could they be?

Elizabeth took Enid's arm. "Look, Enid, if you see any of the guys, let me know, all right?"

"Sure, Liz," Enid agreed.

"And don't let them leave, OK?" Elizabeth said. "Tell them—tell them . . ." She bit her lip, unable to think of a reason the boys shouldn't be allowed to leave.

"Don't worry, Liz, I'll think of something," Enid said, waving her away.

"Thanks, Enid," Elizabeth whispered.

"There's Jessica over by the refreshment table," Enid said, pointing across the room. "Maybe she's with Ken."

Elizabeth rushed off, practically flying toward her twin. "Excuse me, excuse me," she mumbled, bumping into people and jostling her way through the crowd.

"Jessica!" she cried as she arrived at the table. Jessica was standing with Lila and Amy, and they were all holding plates of food and laughing. Lila and Amy were dressed as geisha girls, wearing elegant long pale-blue silk dresses and satin slippers. To complement their outfits, they were both holding beautiful, elaborately decorated Japanese masks on sticks.

Jessica looked up in astonishment as Elizabeth slid toward her.

"What's up, Liz?" Jessica asked. "Are you being chased?"

Elizabeth pulled her aside. "Where's Ken?"

Jessica shrugged. "I was wondering that myself. I haven't seen him since I arrived."

"Do you have any idea where he went?" Elizabeth demanded.

Jessica shook her head. "I haven't got a clue. I was planning to stick by his side all evening, but before I knew it, he was gone."

Elizabeth's heart sank. "Jessica, they're all gone," she said.

"They're probably arguing with the Palisades guys somewhere," Jessica guessed.

"I'm calling the police," Elizabeth announced.

"Oh, c'mon," Jessica scoffed. "Don't you think that's a little extreme? They're just going to insult each other for a while."

"I don't think so," Elizabeth replied. "I've got a feeling in my bones. Something really bad is going to happen."

"You went to all this trouble to have this dance, and now you want to ruin it?" Jessica shook her head. "Liz, you're crazy."

But Elizabeth didn't care what Jessica thought. She had created this situation; now she had to do something to resolve it.

Elizabeth ran off in search of a phone. "If you can find them, tell Ken and Todd that the police are on their way!" she shouted over her shoulder to her twin.

194

Chapter 13

Ken bounced on the balls of his feet, the blood pulsing through his veins. He flexed his muscles and clenched his fists, ready to spring at Greg McMullen. He wanted to slam his fist into Greg's jaw and send him flying to the ground. He felt like beating him to a pulp and making him cry for mercy. Ken had never experienced such violent urges. It was as if he had become a totally different person.

The Sweet Valley guys and Palisades guys were facing off in the lot behind the warehouse. They had found an emergency exit and had slipped out the back, throwing off their masks and their jackets. Now they were all in jeans and T-shirts. *Just man-to-man*, Ken thought in satisfaction, eager for the showdown to begin.

Rain was coming down in a steady drizzle, and the atmosphere was eerily silent. Since they had left the warehouse, nobody had said a word. The guys were sizing each other up, waiting for somebody to make the first move.

Ken's stomach coiled in fear as he looked at the opposition. Things didn't look good. They were a mean-looking group. He recognized two of them as the guys that had been with McMullen after the football game. Standing next to them was a burly punk with short-cropped hair and a face like a bull. The guy next to him was tall and skinny, with stringy red hair and a cratered face.

Ken had never seen the one who appeared to be the leader. He was huge, and his blue eyes were dangerously cold.

The next thing Ken knew, the guy's fist was heading straight toward his face.

Jessica pushed open the heavy steel door at the side of the warehouse and stepped outside into the rain. "Ken?" she called into the dark night. "Todd?" Even though she scoffed at Elizabeth for calling the police, she had a bad feeling about the boys' disappearance, too. If she could find the guys and let them know the police were coming, maybe she could prevent them from getting into a fight.

If they aren't fighting already, Jessica thought anxiously, shivering in the cold. *I'm sure they're only arguing.* Rain was falling on her exposed shoulders, and air was rushing at her bare back.

She wrapped her arms around herself and walked quickly along the side of the building. A heel sunk into the wet grass, and Jessica stumbled to the ground. She wiped her hands on her dress, then pulled off her pumps. Holding a shoe in each hand, she ran in her bare feet to the parking lot.

"Is anybody here?" she called, weaving through the cars. The words echoed in the deserted lot. Jessica squeezed through a row of vehicles, making her way to the back of the lot where Ken had parked. She scanned the cars and quickly found Ken's white Toyota. It was still there. But where was Ken?

"Ken! Todd!" Jessica called again, cupping her hands around her mouth so the sound would carry. The names bounced off the cars and reverberated in the empty space. Jessica ran across the front of the warehouse to the other side, getting more and more worried as the seconds ticked by.

The right side of the warehouse was an unkempt lot, overgrown with grass and shrubs. Jessica waded across it, knee-high in weeds. A spider crawled up her arm, and she swatted it off. Her spine tingled as she felt the weeds tickling her legs. There could be poisonous spiders hidden in the tall grass. Or rattlesnakes. Or rats.

Feeling spooked, Jessica increased her speed. She crossed the lot quickly and ran around the side of the building to the back. She was in a gravel lot. Jessica leaned against the building until her breathing slowed. Slipping her feet back into her shoes, she walked quickly across the gravel.

Then she stopped in her tracks. A horrible scene was playing itself out across the lot. The guys were engaged in a brutal fight. All she could see was a twisted mass of arms and fists. The only sounds that could be heard were groans of pain and thumps of fists as they made contact with flesh.

Jessica felt woozy and leaned against the wall for support. Then she panicked, worried about Ken. She ran toward the fight.

First she saw the guy she recognized as the Palisades linebacker punching Todd in the stomach. Todd was bent over double, trying to guard against the blows.

Stifling a scream, she ran forward. Then she stopped, gasping in horror. Ken was flat on his back on the ground, his face so covered in blood, she could hardly make out his features. His body was perfectly still.

Jessica let out a bloodcurdling scream. "Ken!" she cried, running toward him.

She looked up at his attacker and her knees went weak.

It was Christian.

As his smoky blue eyes reached hers, Jessica sank to her knees. She covered her face, sobbing.

In the distance she could hear the wail of sirens and the sound of feet running in every direction. She felt cold, hard gravel against her cheek as she slumped to the ground.

Then nothing. Blackness.

The rivalry between Sweet Valley High and Palisades High continues to escalate . . . with Jessica and Elizabeth caught in the middle. When the smoke clears, will the twins ever be forgiven? Find out in the second book of this fiery three-part miniseries, **The High School Wars.**

Bantam Books in the Sweet Valley High series
Ask your bookseller for the books you have missed

SIGN UP FOR THE SWEET VALLEY HIGH® FAN CLUB!

Hey, girls! Get all the gossip on Sweet Valley High's® most popular teenagers when you join our fantastic Fan Club! As a member, you'll get all of this really cool stuff:

- Membership Card with your own personal Fan Club ID number
- A Sweet Valley High® Secret Treasure Box
- Sweet Valley High® Stationery
- Official Fan Club Pencil (for secret note writing!)
- Three Bookmarks
- A "Members Only" Door Hanger
- Two Skeins of J. & P. Coats® Embroidery Floss with flower barrette instruction leaflet
- Two editions of *The Oracle* newsletter
- Plus exclusive Sweet Valley High® product offers, special savings, contests, and much more!

Be the first to find out what Jessica & Elizabeth Wakefield are up to by joining the Sweet Valley High® Fan Club for the one-year membership fee of only $6.25 each for U.S. residents, $8.25 for Canadian residents (U.S. currency). Includes shipping & handling.

Send a check or money order (do not send cash) made payable to "Sweet Valley High® Fan Club" along with this form to:

SWEET VALLEY HIGH® FAN CLUB, BOX 3919-B, SCHAUMBURG, IL 60168-3919

NAME_____
         (Please print clearly)

ADDRESS_____

CITY_____ STATE_____ ZIP_____
                                                (Required)

AGE_____ BIRTHDAY_____ /_____ /_____